P9-DVB-216

And He Tells the Little Horse the Whole Story

WITHDRAWN
UTSA Libraries

Johns Hopkins: Poetry and Fiction

John T. Irwin, General Editor

Guy Davenport, *Da Vinci's Bicycle: Ten Stories*

John Hollander, *"Blue Wine" and Other Poems*

Robert Pack, *Waking to My Name: New and Selected Poems*

Stephen Dixon, *Fourteen Stories*

Philip Dacey, *The Boy under the Bed*

Jack Matthews, *Dubious Persuasions*

Guy Davenport, *Tatlin!*

Wyatt Prunty, *The Times Between*

Barry Spacks, *Spacks Street: New and Selected Poems*

Joe Ashby Porter, *The Kentucky Stories*

Gibbons Ruark, *Keeping Company*

Stephen Dixon, *Time to Go*

Jack Matthews, *Crazy Women*

David St. John, *Hush*

Jean McGarry, *Airs of Providence*

Wyatt Prunty, *What Women Know, What Men Believe*

Adrien Stoutenberg, *Land of Superior Mirages: New and Selected Poems*

John Hollander, *In Time and Place*

Jack Matthews, *Ghostly Populations*

Charles Martin, *Steal the Bacon*

Jean McGarry, *The Very Rich Hours*

Steve Barthelme, *And He Tells the Little Horse the Whole Story*

And He Tells the Little Horse the Whole Story

Steve Barthelme

The Johns Hopkins University Press

Baltimore and London

This book has been brought to publication with the generous assistance of the G. Harry Pouder Fund and the Albert Dowling Trust.

© 1987 The Johns Hopkins University Press
All rights reserved
Printed in the United States of America

The Johns Hopkins University Press, 701 West 40th Street,
Baltimore, Maryland 21211
The Johns Hopkins Press Ltd., London

The paper used in this publication meets the minimum requirements of American National Standard for Information Sciences—Permanence of Paper for Printed Library Materials, ANSI Z39.48-1984. ∞

Some stories in this volume appeared in the following periodicals, to whose editors grateful acknowledgment is made: *Florida Review:* "Zach"; *Massachusetts Review:* "Mrs. Sims," "Michael"; *New Delta Review:* "Liars"; *North American Review:* "Here You Are"; *Transatlantic Review:* "The Friend," "Samaritan"; and *Yale Review:* "Zorro."

Acknowledgment is also made to the PEN Syndicated Fiction Project for "Black Jack" and "Stoner's Lament."

Library of Congress Cataloging-in-Publication Data
Barthelme, Steve.
 And he tells the little horse the whole story.

 (Johns Hopkins, poetry and fiction)
 I. Title. II. Series.
PS3552.A7635A8 1987   813'.54   87-45477
ISBN 0-8018-3543-7

LIBRARY
The University of Texas
at San Antonio

To my mother and father

To my mother and father

Iona is silent for a moment, then continues:

"That's how it is, my old horse. There's no more Kuzma Ionitch. He has left us to live, and he went off pop. Now let's say, you had a foal, you were the foal's mother, and suddenly, let's say, that foal went and left you to live after him. It would be sad, wouldn't it?"

The little horse munches, listens, and breathes over its master's hand. . . .

Iona's feelings are too much for him, and he tells the little horse the whole story.

Anton Chekhov, "The Lament"

Contents

Black Jack   1

Mrs. Sims   8

Here You Are   18

Stoner's Lament   26

Liars   34

Zach   41

Failing All Else   47

Michael   54

Get-together   64

The Friend   70

Chat   77

Samaritan   82

That's No Reason   92

Their House   101

Beach   112

Zorro   124

Problematical Species   136

And He Tells the Little Horse the Whole Story

Black Jack

When the word *macho* became a popular term of disparagement, a few years ago, I thought it was funny. That was the word my mother had always used to describe my father. She used it admiringly. *Macho hombre*. To me he was just a big blotched man sitting on a wicker chair, looking out over the weeds and rusty barrels piled up in a lot across the highway.

When I knew him he was an old man, near seventy, and not happy. I was a child, eleven or twelve, and this was eighteen years ago, and the story he told occurred more than sixty years before that. I don't really remember what he looked like, except that I have a child's memory of his wrinkled, blotched skin and his baldness and the disarray of his teeth, some missing, some crooked, some brown. I remember one other thing, his hands grinding into the thick fur at the neck and shoulders of an old gray and black and white cat. The cat resembled him somewhat, except that it smiled, or whatever it is they do. That picture has stayed with me for almost twenty years and has defined for me, in part, what it is to be a man.

It did not occur to me then, and I do not know what I think about it now, that he might have been selfish to have a child when he was nearing sixty, or that he was lonely or unhappy, or that it might be odd for a child to have of his father only a memory of bad teeth, an image of a contented cat, and a sixty-year-old story about a trip on a railroad train. By the time I was sitting with him on the porch of that house in Lake Charles he had been divorced from my mother for six or seven years, and as we lived in El Paso and he in Louisiana, we rarely saw him; a year later, he was dead.

He knew how to stroke a cat. The cat was content, and self-contained, but it's his hands I remember, measured, slow, expert. We were sitting in wicker chairs. I had just arrived, on the train, and he was telling me about a train trip he had taken.

"I was seven, much younger than you are now," he said. "I was going east to visit my Daddy's family, who lived in Baltimore. His father, your great-granddaddy—they called him 'Mister,' just 'Mister'—had made money in railroading, but sold out too early. But to us, they were filthy rich. They lived in a big house, my Daddy told me, with servants, and white tablecloths on every table, lobster at every meal. Rockefellers and Vanderbilts came to call. My Daddy was a great liar." He laughed. "Once he told me about a clock he had had when he was a kid. He told me there was this tiny man inside, a live man—" He held up his fingers, three inches apart. "—and this man was one of only a hundred in the whole world, so they were worth more than gold; and you had to feed them chickadee eggs, and steaks as thin as paper. Anyway, on the hour the tiny man would run out on the balcony of the clock and yell, 'Cuckoo! cuckoo!'" My father laughed and laughed, rocking the cat on his lap, but still petting it. "He told me that he had sold the clock and that that had made old Mister so mad he sent him to Texas, as punishment. That was why, you see, we lived in a little bitch-cold A-frame on Calle de Oro in El Paso when we were really filthy rich with a railroad fortune coming our way and a thirty-room mansion in the great city of Baltimore. He was a terrific liar.

"When I got to Baltimore, the house was more like seven or eight rooms. No servants. No tablecloths. If a Rockefeller ever saw the place, it was to pick up the rent. My granddaddy was a nice enough man, old by that time. When you get old, you get nice, I guess. He had a hickory cane, and he would sit out on the lawn of that house with five or six other old men and they'd chew tobacco and spit, all afternoon. Mister did have friends. After he railroaded, he gambled. Made a good living at it, too. After he gambled for a living, he gambled for fun. The thing about cards is that when you get enough amateurs—people holding kickers and drawing to inside straights—in the game, the odds just go out the window. And when you get old, it's too much trouble to remember cards and things like that. At least, too much trouble just to win money."

Then my own father stopped stroking the cat and looked at me, just stared. "You know, that's what I want. I'd like five or six guys to play cards with. And to sit out here and soak up the sun and talk and spit tobacco juice out over the railing." He shook his head, slowly.

"So anyway, when I got to Baltimore, they lived in this little house. I didn't believe it at first. I thought I was being kidnapped. Somehow they finally convinced me that they were in point of fact my grand-parents. She was a tall woman with a pair of moles, here—" He touched the side of his face. "Said they were 'beauty marks.' And she could fry chicken like no one else in the world. I was there about two weeks, and every morning she'd ask me what I wanted for dinner, and every morning, after the first night, I'd say 'Fried chicken.' Old Mis-ter must have been happy to see me go, all that chicken. She made fried chicken that was the equal of the *migas* your momma used to make me before we got married. And that, my boy, is king's praise. She still make those *migas?* With peppers she grew herself? *Muy malo.* Doubt I could eat them now."

I was eleven and I didn't like it when he talked about my mother. Our mutual acquaintance. He was so much a stranger that it seemed evil, or dirty. It was then that I would notice his wrinkled, blotchy skin, or his teeth, and my mother was to my eyes something too per-fect and too delicate for conversation, or comment, olive-skinned, soft-spoken, and hideously vulnerable. A woman. Even though his voice was slow with regret and his eyes were soft almost with tears, I could not bear it. The idea that I was the issue of their love, the irony of thinking him dirty when he talked about her, was just one other thing that escaped me. She was fragile. He was old. But he knew how to pet the cat, and the cat liked the hardness of his grip, the strength in his seventy-year-old fingers, and the old man knew how hard was too hard. But I didn't want him to talk about her. One of her boy-friends had once thrown me out a window, first-floor window, and I lay beside a pyracantha, picking its thorns out of my jeans and look-ing at the dirty red berries, and I remember thinking, triumphantly, "That's the end of him," and of course it was.

"Anyway," he said, "I was going to tell you about the first train I ever rode. It was a big deal in those days. Southern Pacific. They got me up in the coat and tie—I was going to visit the rich folks, you see. And they took me downtown to the station. I was about six or seven. I was going halfway across the country, by myself, and my mother was crying, and there were lots of other people all around, and I couldn't understand why she was crying. You never met her but if you had, you'd know she wasn't the type to cry—big tough woman and no nonsense about her. I used to watch her gut the deer my Daddy'd bring home sometimes. He'd hang it from a tree and she'd go out there with a knife and cut. Anyway, she was crying. And right about time to board the train we were standing out by it, by the tracks, they had these long wooden walks in between the trains and everybody was standing out there. The train conductor walks up and she grabbed him by the arm, right in front of me, and starts giving him instructions. She tells him who I am, and how old I am. By this time everybody else is already on board the train. My Daddy's wait-ing. There are the four of us standing out there and the train's crank-ing up, blowing, and people are looking out the windows at us. She tells the conductor—this elderly gent with glasses—that I'm chang-ing trains, at St. Louis. She writes it down for him, tells him which train goes to Baltimore, which he probably knew. There weren't that many, in those days. Then she tells him again that I'm seven years old, and she tells him to *walk* me to the train, when we got to St. Louis, and put me on it, and gives him a silver dollar. By this time, I can't stand it any more, so I step up on the train, turn back and stare at her."

I could feel his anger, carried for sixty years, the child who did not want to be a child, or at least, did not want to be smaller than any one else, and in his voice was the child's sense that the whole train was waiting on him and on his mother to slip the conductor a silver dollar, because he needed the help which he knew he did not need.

"That stopped her," my father said. "She rushed over and hugged me, and my Daddy shook my hand, and the conductor nodded to me, and then to them and that was that. The train smelled. Everything smelled in those days. It was summer and it was hot, but beneath the smell of people, the train smelled like oil and grease and steel. I felt great. I picked a seat where nobody'd sit beside me, and after he took my ticket, the conductor didn't come around much. I changed seats a couple times to avoid him, so he didn't get a fix on me.

"The train went north, then to Fort Worth and Dallas. The first night he gave me a pillow and blanket. He was a decent old guy, but my mother had made him my enemy. I wasn't friendly, but I couldn't think of a reason not to take the pillow. But I wouldn't take the blanket. I slept in my coat and tie. He probably thought I was the world's biggest brat." My father laughed. "I probably was the world's biggest brat.

"The first day was all desert, like east of the city, but the next morning it was rolling country and it was green and I had never seen anything like it. Miles and miles of it like a rug. It wasn't much of a train I guess, but sometimes we'd cross a bridge and you could look out a window and see the rest of it, the locomotive up ahead and the cars in front curving around, and I felt like somebody in a book, somebody they write books about. My Daddy'd said Black Jack Pershing was on this train, and I was looking for him. I was already in school then, a year ahead of the boys my age."

The old man was proud of this, too, which I thought was insufferably foolish pride and held against him for the longest time, until much later when I realized that I could remember test scores (which weren't all that spectacular, anyway) from high school when other people could not. My whole life seems sometimes like a process of forgiving other people, principally my father, but my mother and others as well, forgiving them when I find myself, later, doing exactly the same thing.

It was also odd to hear him say "boys" that way. "The boys my age . . . " It made me feel uncomfortable, to have this tired man talking about some time so distant as to be unknowable, almost ridiculous, when he was like me and the people I knew, small, akin to the way he must have felt in that El Paso train station in 1911 or whenever it was. What I think now, at thirty, is, You can forgive, but don't you ever forget?

"We went through Dallas, and Oklahoma City, and Tulsa, and Springfield. You don't hear much about Springfield any more. In those days, it was a big deal, I don't know why. My Daddy'd talked about it. He'd been there. He'd been everywhere. But that was

Springfield in Illinois. This was Springfield in Missouri. I don't know . . . "

He was confused, just for a moment, rubbing his face with his hand, and suddenly I felt in danger of some kind, I was afraid of him. And I remembered what he'd said about the friends he wanted for his poker game, and that made him seem more dangerous, and I was glad he didn't have them, but I felt cruel at the same time. I felt guilty for his loneliness. I was eleven. I was confused, too.

"Anyway," he said. "Well, hell. To me when the conductor came along shouting 'Next stop, Springfield,' I felt like a real man of the world. For about thirty seconds. I asked him how long it was to St. Louis. He told me a hundred miles or two hundred miles, or whatever it was, and that was all right, I could figure it out, I had been reading a timetable all the way from El Paso. But he looked at me, and said, 'Don't worry, we'll get you on your way. We won't send you to Chicago.' And he smiled. First chance I got, I moved to another car. I slept a little, it was nighttime. Out the windows you'd see a light and then a little further on you'd see another light, far off. Lots of lights when we got into St. Louis, lights for miles and miles. I waited and went into another car. There was nobody in it. It felt strange, rocking through the city alone in that railroad car, where all the empty seats looked like people, and looking out the windows, sometimes a building or some rock would pass and I'd jump back, because it was so close, and then there'd be more lights. I stayed there, and waited for the train to stop.

"When it finally did stop, it was easy. I waited for the people to start getting off the train and then beat it for the door to the car. I saw him coming through the next car, looking, and I jumped down and ran. I had a little hand suitcase and I'd been carrying it with me, from car to car. I just went back into the station there. I looked up and got the name and number of the train for Baltimore, found the track, and walked up to the conductor. This one was wearing the same blue suit, but he was a boy, he didn't seem much older than I was, must have been eighteen, but he didn't seem so. You know what he said?" You could almost watch the old man remember; he took his time. "He said, 'Yes *sir.*' " My father smiled; the cat was asleep in his lap.

My father was seventy years old when he told me this story. I have never since seen anyone so proud. He didn't need any help. He didn't need anybody else. He would do it all himself. He didn't even need my mother.

I am thirty but I understand what he told me. I would like, myself, to have card games. We could get Black Jack Pershing to play, and old Mister, and Mister's boy, my grandfather, would tell outrageous lies about tiny men who live in clocks, and my father would laugh, and nobody would tell him, or me for that matter, that we had made the same mistake our whole lives long.

Mrs. Sims

It's spring. We stand on our lawns, looking down, four of us in a row, separated each from the next by maybe fifty feet of driveways, hedges, trees. The only one I know is Mrs. Sims, next-door, in this line now that her husband is dead. The Augustine grass is yellow, ragged, dead in spots. There are twigs and leaves.

Mrs. Sims is past seventy, but she frowns at the grass just the way Mr. Sims did, more skillfully than the rest of us who are all younger, and male. Her lawn looks better than any of ours. Since her husband died I've done the heavy work on it, but she tells me what to do, and when.

"Time to get that thatch out," Mrs. Sims'll say, as we're standing on my driveway late in February, early in March, and we get the rakes and drag the dead runners out of the yellow grass. I finish first, so I wander over and finish hers too. When she waters, I water, even if it's December. Some winters are dry.

"I remember Milstead didn't water one winter," she says, "and the next spring he had a tractor over there, scraped the whole yard up. He was sure he had Augustine decline. Willard laughed and laughed, he thought that was real funny. Willard said, 'Milstead thinks he's got a virus, but that grass just died of thirst.' " Milstead lives on the other side of her. Willard was Mr. Sims' name.

There's a bare area in her yard now that's grown to about twelve feet square. The bare place is on the other side of a low hedge running beside my driveway, so I don't see it except when I'm over there. But it bothers her. Her daughter is coming, the daughter who married the doctor, and the lawn needs to be shipshape. She explains this to me on the driveway one Saturday.

"You'll like Mary Beth," Mrs. Sims says. "She's a picture. Has this great big head of black hair. And this little bitty husband. Billy, just between us—" She puts her wrinkled, spotted hand on my arm. "Just between us, he's a twerp. Some kind of bone doctor, a chiropodist or something, in California. Seems like he could just as well be a chiropodist in Texas. All I know is he makes money, and he's a twerp." She looks away. "I'm terrible," she says, giggling. "Truth to tell, he's good-looking. But you see why I've got to get my house in shape. She'll want me to move out there and live in their hot tub." When she laughs the lines in her face look like a spiderweb.

"You ordered some of this—what's it called?"

"Floratan," she says. "I was thinking about that new Raleigh, but they told me they want five dollars a yard for it. I said thank you very much."

"I guess we need to turn all this dirt today?"

"If you have time," Mrs. Sims says. "Or I could just wet the sod down, and we could do it any time. The men should have been here with it by now."

"Today's all right. Let me get into my working clothes. I'll need your pitchfork."

"Honey," she says. "That's a spading fork. A pitchfork is for hay."

"Spading fork," I say.

I go back inside my house. At first I can't find my best old jeans but then I remember leaving them in the workshop, which is actually the back bedroom. The sawdust swirls as I open the door. There's a chest I've been working on, cleaning it up to refinish. Maybe next weekend, I think.

A small flatbed truck has arrived in front of Mrs. Sims' house and two guys in overalls toss big rectangles of sod off the back onto her lawn. It travels six or seven feet in the air over the sidewalk. I can hear the thudding through my closed living room windows. She'll want to move it first thing, I think, watching.

I get back outside as they're finishing up. The grass on the sod is yellowing, matted down. I expected it bright green and perfect. The four of us stand on the sidewalk by the truck, and the bigger of the two guys reaches out with an invoice. I take it. It's illegible.

"What's this here?"

He leans over me to look. "Fifteen dollars," he says. "Delivery." His breath's bad and he needs a shave. "Look, I just drive the truck. You coulda picked it up."

Mrs. Sims takes the invoice, looks it over quickly, fills out her check. After they leave, she says, "Don't get upset, Billy. They put fifteen dollars on everything, nowadays. It seems that way. I could have picked it up." She shrugs. "The Incredible Hulk," she says. "Wasn't he?"

She's in a blue cotton dress, straw hat, tennis shoes. Skinny. The spading fork is leaning against the side of her house, near the end of the porch. She gets it and heads for the bare area beside the hedge. I wait for her to turn and look at me, and when she does I take over the fork. She walks toward the street, the sod. "It'll kill the grass," she says. "I don't know why he couldn't have just thrown it on the sidewalk."

I dig while she's moving the crumbling sod onto the sidewalk. Someone honks from the street, but when I look up she's waving at a car already past.

The ground is softer than I would have guessed but somehow that makes digging it up a little harder. You have to go deeper. There are roots in it too, and the prongs of the fork catch in them every other time, so turning the dirt takes a long time.

"Just break it up, honey," Mrs. Sims says, from behind me, "you don't have to atomize it." Now she's sitting in a deck chair just past the end of the concrete porch, worn out. "I'll get you some gloves. Do you want an iced tea?"

I nod, and spear the fork into the ground, twice. The second time, it stays upright. Big red blisters have grown up in the middle of my palms.

"Are you trying to get straight A's or something?" she says. She used to be a schoolteacher. "You should have some gloves." She disappears down her porch, and I hear the screen slam behind her. I sit on the lawn and take my shirt off, wiping my forehead with it. Digging is a lot harder work than I remembered. The sun feels good on my back, the way it does every spring, after the cold winter, before the heat of the summer.

She's gone almost twenty minutes, and I begin to wonder if maybe I should have moved the sod. But, if I had, she would've been digging. Her cat, W.T., wanders down the porch and jumps off the end, then crosses to where I'm sitting. He's black, with gold eyes. W.T. stands for "Willard Two." Mrs. Sims told me her daughter said that was a horrible name.

W.T. brushes against me, feeling friendly. He humps his back to get full benefit of the petting, then walks away. I watch him stumble on the broken ground and disappear under the hedge. Mrs. Sims is coming down the porch with two bags of peat moss from her garage. The bags are white plastic, square, and they look heavy.

"Throw some of this on there," she says. "I don't know that it works, but the man in the paper swears by it. There's wood in the top, watch the tacks."

One of the bags has a hole near the bottom where it says "1 Cubic Foot Product of Canada," and it's leaking, so I rip it there and throw the brown pulp over the ground I've dug up. It's like throwing dust, the peat moss drifts.

Mrs. Sims sits in the deck chair. "Did you see any of those red worms? Should be a lot over there where the leaves pile up, along the hedge."

"Yeah, a lot of the big ones." I've only seen one, but I assume there are worms. "Move over here," I say, pointing.

She shakes her head, puzzled. "If you want to quit for today, Billy, it's okay," she says. "I'd like to move that tallow tree, though, before you clean up. I'd like it about a yard closer to the house."

The tree is across the lawn, next to her driveway, about twelve feet high and the diameter of a small utility pole. "You're kidding," I say.

"Who me?" she says, and laughs.

I pull on the gloves she's brought and turn the rest of the dirt, taking a more careless attitude, which makes the work go faster. After I spread the rest of the peat moss and run a rake over the whole thing, it's almost dark, and my hands hurt. We look at each other.

"Damn. I forgot your iced tea," she says, frowning. "Damn."

"I'll have some next time." I take the spading fork, rake, and gloves and put them in the corner of her garage, then cross the porch and wave to her as I reach the opening onto my driveway at the end of the hedge. She's at the street with the hose, wetting the sod. She waves.

I don't see her on Sunday, she never comes outside, and I'm reluctant to knock, so the sodding takes the next week, partially because I can only help in the evenings, and partially because Mrs. Sims has a design in mind.

We cut the new sod in ten-inch squares and then plant it with two-inch corridors of bare earth running in between in both directions. A tattersall pattern. The first pieces I put down all have to be picked up and planted down below the level of the dirt. "Come summer, I don't want a bunch of canals," she says. "The dirt'll pack." We finish on Friday.

"It looks like hell," Mrs. Sims says, as we're standing on the end of her porch. "Pardon my French. I should have just done it solid, but Willard did the back this way and it came out perfect."

"Looks okay. Give it some time."

"Time is what I don't have enough of, honey," she says, taking her hat off, wiping her forehead. The hat is pale straw with a ring of overweight horses woven into the crown. Her bluish hair holds the imprint of the hat, like a permanent.

"I'm baking you some cookies," she says. "Come inside."

By the time I sit down, after washing my hands, she already has a plate of hot chocolate-chip cookies on the small table between us. The cookies are perfect circles.

The house is ordinary from the outside but the interior is full of aging modern furniture. There are swooping armchairs with laminated wood arms and the fabric gone, a big rosewood Eames chair and stool with the black leather worn red in places, tables with chipped glass and nicked chrome. New white shag carpet. An extraordinary squat black deco clock with brass hands sits in a bookcase.

"These come in a roll," she says, picking up a cookie. She's sitting in the rosewood armchair. "The frozen kind. As good as I can make myself, and they're a whole lot easier."

"They're good," I say.

W.T. jumps for the low table, catching the edge, and his back legs go into a furious churning. He makes it, and heads for the plate of cookies.

"Willard," Mrs. Sims says, sternly.

The cat stops motionless, staring.

"Not good enough," she says, in the same tone, and W.T. jumps back to the floor.

"Now tell me," Mrs. Sims says, picking a black cat hair from the table, "are you going to marry that pretty little girl I see you with? The one that yells, 'Bill! It's nigh-un o'clock!' She's one of your students?"

"Was," I say.

Mrs. Sims shakes her head. "Wasn't done in my day. Although I'll admit it passed through my mind more than a few times. My students, I mean. Some of the other teachers dabbled."

"Dabbled is a pretty good word for it."

She laughs, rubbing at mud on her small, bony knee. When she notices me watching she says, "Spots," and looks then at her arm. She feigns brushing the arm with her hand, looks up with steel-gray eyes. "Spots. They're a curse."

On my way back to my house, I check the sod, which doesn't look at all bad in the light from the streetlights.

It's dark outside but darker inside. I flip the kitchen switch and nothing happens. "Well, okay," I tell myself, out loud. On the way to the living room I think I hear something and stop, but then there's nothing after so I get to the couch and feel for the lamp on the table next to it. The lamp doesn't come on either. "Give me a break," I say. Across from me the floor creaks and I jump, kicking the coffee table, as someone speaks.

"Bang bang," she says.

"Julia?"

"You were expecting, maybe, someone else?"

I rest, sitting back on the couch, straining to see her, in one of the chairs across the room, until she shines a flashlight in my eyes.

"Bang bang. Your precious belt sander is in the sink. Under water," she says. "Psssssssst. Bang, bang. I was going to throw the drill in there, too, but I couldn't find it in the dark. It was just like a little speedboat, the sander I mean, before it exploded."

I stare at her. She is pretty, extremely pretty, but not at all little—

a shade under six feet. She is a "girl." Two out of three isn't bad.

"Don't take it so hard," she says. "They'll put them on sale again. I saw you, out in the yard, when I came. I wished I was her."

"How's Slade, or Howard, or whatever his name is?" I say. "Still going to put you in the band? Make you a star?"

"He's at his sexual peak." She picks up her purse and throws a key on the couch. "Here, give this to Ma Kettle," she says, starting for the kitchen. She stops at the door, looks down at the flashlight in her hand.

"Jule—"

She throws the flashlight and it twirls end over end like a baton, past my head, hitting the wall, and goes out. "Don't call me that," she says, in the dark. "You have no right."

She leaves the door open, I can hear the traffic. Out the living room windows I watch the highlights swing in her long, waist-length hair as she walks across the lawn, talking to herself. Then I remember my belt sander.

Three weeks later, Mrs. Sims calls and invites me to dinner with her daughter and son-in-law, at her house, the following Saturday. I run into her on Tuesday afternoon, too, out surveying the grass we planted, and she says, "You're coming this weekend, aren't you?"

I nod. "Looks pretty good here, doesn't it?"

"Oh, it does not," she says. "I've got a man coming to mow it. I thought of asking you, but I want to save you for important things, like spreading weed-killer and Fertilome."

"You've finally given up? Mowing it yourself I mean?" A black look comes over her face. "Just too damn hot now," I say, hurriedly. "When is Mary Beth getting in?"

"They don't want me in California," she says. "They're going overseas." What passes through my mind is, Why is she telling me this? and instantly I feel this terrible shame, which she makes worse by noticing, by saying, "But then, you've got your own troubles."

"Damn, you don't want to go to California anyway. They don't have lawns there, it's paved solid."

"Don't blaspheme," she says.

Mrs. Sims is in a silk dress, royal blue, stooped over, uncomfortable. The sleeves swish when she moves her arms. Dinner is roast beef. Her hands shake as she carries the heavy platter to the table. Mary Beth tries to take the platter from her, but she stops and fixes her daughter with a stare. The cat, W.T., is underfoot; I'm afraid he'll trip her.

"It's a rib-eye roast," Mrs. Sims says. "I hope it's good."

Mary Beth is plain with a big square face, compensates with make-up. Gold eyeshadow and rouge, liberally applied. I think I hear Mrs. Sims tell her, in the kitchen, that she looks like a "gargoyle." Mary Beth's husband, Dan, is short and handsome, an Irishman with a black moustache. For some reason, he reminds me of an airline pilot.

"You're a history teacher, Bill?" he says, at the table. "Professor, I mean."

"Associate," I say. Mrs. Sims has introduced me as Bill, although she's never called me anything but "Billy."

"History's really important," Dan says. "Don't know it, doomed to repeat it."

"Yes, it's so historical," Mary Beth says, setting down her fork. She eats crisply, like someone in a movie. I notice that we are all eating that way, or trying to. The roast is rare and rich as candy and there's Yorkshire pudding.

"Dan is a chiropodist," Mrs. Sims says, to me.

"Orthopedist, Mother," Mary Beth says, with raised eyebrows. "A bone specialist."

"Well," Mrs. Sims says, "they all sound like some kind of grasshopper to me. I remember when we just had doctors."

"You had a lot more sick and dying people, too," Mary Beth says. "Your own father died at forty because those simple doctors of yours didn't know about streptomycin."

"Not at table, Mary," Mrs. Sims says.

Mary Beth looks at me, assumes a confidential tone. "Mother's just tired," she says. "She's a little cross." I don't know whether to smile or not, so I reach for my water glass. Mrs. Sims is angry, but Dan interrupts her.

"They do sort of sound like grasshoppers," he says, laughing. "We do."

W.T. is on the floor beside Mrs. Sims' chair. "Willard," she says. "Shoo." The cat is trying, limp-wristed, to pull one of his paws from the shag carpet. Mrs. Sims says, "He never does this. He never begs."

"Dogs beg, Mother," Mary Beth says. "Cats don't beg."

The cat finally disentangles his claws from the carpet, and stands at attention, gold eyes aglow. He looks like he is begging.

After dinner Mary Beth and I wash dishes. She keeps her mother out of the kitchen by bringing up investments, which is a sideline of Dan's. He almost chokes when Mrs. Sims reveals several thousand dollars in a passbook savings account. "It's five and three-quarter percent!" he says. "They're robbing you."

"I know," Mrs. Sims says, "but they're very nice over there."

Mary Beth rinses the dishes and I arrange them in the dishwasher, which is new, with plastic racks a strange color somewhere between green and blue. Mary Beth talks about her mother, too loud. I nod toward the living room doorway, but she ignores me.

"You know what she does all day long?" Mary Beth says. "She watches *television*. All night, too. I call, and she wants to talk about 'Dynasty.' Or the ads. She imbibes that mindless garbage all day long. And then she *buys* the junk. Look at this."

She puts a soapy plate down next to the sink, reaches up and opens a cabinet door, then slams it. Inside are colored cardboard boxes, cartoon characters, E.T. the Extraterrestrial is on one I think. I feel rotten for looking. "Well?" Mary Beth says.

She doesn't give me a chance to answer, which is fortunate because I can't think of anything to say.

"And the furniture! I never liked modern much, but My God, it's rotting away. She could at least have it redone, it's not a question of money. Can't she see it? She's argumentative, she forgets things, and the way she drives, My God. I worry about her all the time."

"I wondered about the furniture," I say. "I wondered whether she likes it. I mean whether it was your father's idea, originally?"

"She *loves* it." We're through with the dishes. Mary Beth slaps the dishwasher closed, turns it on. It's loud.

She leans her hip against the counter. "Are you married?" she says, and when I hold up my hand, showing no ring, she says, "If you aren't married, you wouldn't know what it's like to worry about someone, I mean worry yourself sick, all the time."

"I had parents," I say.

"Oh, I'm sorry," she says.

We join Dan and Mrs. Sims in the living room. When Mrs. Sims says something about my helping with the lawn, Mary Beth says, "It looks very nice," and Dan says, "Yes, it does."

"It looks nice," Mrs. Sims says, to me. She's in the big rosewood Eames chair, with W.T. "Nice."

"Well, Mother, what do you want me to say? It looks like a golf course? Amber waves of grain? Jesus."

"Don't blaspheme," Mrs. Sims says.

I smile in Mary Beth's direction, to get her attention. "So, how long are you here for?"

"Until day after tomorrow."

"Oh, honey," Mrs. Sims says, "sure you can stay longer than that. I know Dan has to get back. I thought we could go shopping."

"I wish I could, Mother."

A half-hour later I say good night and Mrs. Sims walks me out onto the porch. It's cool. We stand near the end and admire the newly mown sod, which in the blue streetlights appears almost perfect. She steadies herself with a hand on one of the square white posts which bear the roof.

"It was a wonderful dinner," I say. "You'll have to come to dinner at my house, sometime. Let me return the favor."

"Yes," she says, watching the headlights of a car passing down the street. "I'd like that. What will you have?"

"Well, I hadn't thought about it. What do you like?"

She has an idea, she looks up. "You'll think I'm a crazy old lady, Billy."

"Probably," I say. "Probably will."

"Maybe I am," she says. "But I've never been to McDonald's. I'd like to try a Big Mac. Mary says they're awful." She looks tired. The blue dress is too big for her, she's lost in it.

"No, they're good," I say. "They're great. Sort of."

She smiles. "You old liar," she says.

Here You Are

Late, after twelve, Glenna sits on one of the low benches in the waiting area between the bar and tables, leaning forward, with her arms around herself and her Chinese slippers on the floor beside her feet. Her eyes are closed. From where I'm standing, behind the bar, it looks like a photograph.

A couple comes in, I can hear the big door creak before they round the corner and ask if the place is still open. I wave toward the tables. Laughing, they walk back into the darkness. The girl looks at the boy; he calls her a communist. "They don't have enough to eat," she says. After a few minutes, Glenna follows them.

When she gets back, she calls her order: "Scotch, Stoli tonic, Dos Equis, bourbon up, water back." Her hair is in ringlets, natural she says. "You look tired," she says from the end of the bar, leaning on it, smoking a cigarette.

"Couldn't sleep."

"Did you talk to Marianne? About wearing jeans?"

"I did."

"It spoils the illusion," Glenna says.

Glenna understands the bar business. Days, she teaches school. She's thin, with almost no shape at all. When I asked her to choose a dress for the waitresses, she found a pattern in some magazine. The pattern gave her hips, magically.

She takes the drinks out, and when she comes back, sits on the last barstool, looks at her cigarette, which now has a long, droopy ash. She nudges it into the ashtray.

"What if I shower you with cocaine?"

She gives me a schoolteacher frown, as if I've said something I should be ashamed of, something worthy of a guy who owns a bar.

"Glenna. Just a joke."

"Not extremely funny," she says.

"Next one will be extremely funny."

"Is that a promise?" She rests her elbows on the bar, staring at nothing. "I'm just bitchy. All day I talk to eleven-year-olds, all night I talk to drunks. Sometimes I'm standing by a kid's desk and I say something like 'Ready for another?' and do that twinkly smile— The kids look at me like I'm a space invader. Ms. Laser Base." She laughs. Her eyes, all of a sudden, are very wide. Brown eyes.

When Glenna's boyfriend used to pick her up, he would sit at the bar and talk movies. René Clair, Godard, Italians, Germans, Australians. King Vidor. I tried to analyze. She likes long hair, moustaches, short leather jackets, brown. Her boyfriend is a filmmaker. It's a college town, full of filmmakers. His name is Todd. He smokes Gauloises.

In the distance I hear a voice. Glenna is saying, "What are you brooding about?"

"You ask that like a lover," I say, and then hold my hands up. "Sorry."

"You should get more sleep," she says. "You have no respect for your circadian rhythms."

"It's true."

"Are you making fun of me?" There's a brief, instant stare, and then she says, "You wouldn't dare. Would you?" I start to answer, but she's onto something else. "Why'd you quit teaching, Guy?" she says. "Don't you miss it?"

"Daddy left me a chunk of money to open a bar with." She doesn't like this answer. "I ran out of stuff to teach." She watches me run a rag down the top of the bar.

"I know one thing. Two jobs is one job too many. Do you want me to give last call?"

"Not yet."

At one o'clock, Tony comes in and sits at the bar. Glenna's back on the benches. Tony is a regular, big, looks like a lineman. Defensive lineman.

"I'm getting married."

When Tony says something, I never know if it's true or not. I nod, get him a drink.

Tony says, "Remember I found that cat in your parking lot? I took it to the vet; it started sneezing. They gave it a shot, said it was nothing. Feline interruptus or something. Now I've got a damn cat."

"Feline enteritis."

"Oh," Tony says, with a straight face. "I thought it had some kind of sex problem. Are you coming to my party? After I get married?"

"Sure thing."

Tony takes a long look at Glenna, behind him, half-asleep in the waiting area. "Sweet thing."

I nod. "But don't let her hear you say that."

"Anyway," Tony says, "we're gonna have this big party, on the lake. Rented the boat, you know that boat that floats around the lake? The sternwheeler? You can rent it. Tomorrow night."

"You're getting married tomorrow?"

"In August. But the party's tomorrow." Tony rubs a hand over his thinning hair. "I'm going bald. Bald. I need a wife to take care of my cat. You're coming, aren't you? Bring Greta." He jerks his head to the side, indicating Glenna.

"I would if I could," I say. "Who're you marrying?"

"Don't know, some wench."

"Cecilia?"

"Let's watch who we're calling a wench," he says, slapping his empty glass down on the bar. Then he laughs and says, "Yeah. She's real good with cats."

When he lifts the glass again, the base stays on the bar, ice goes all over. "Shit," Tony says. "Christ, I'm sorry." Glenna looks up. I fake a frown.

"Those are imported."

"Christ?" Tony says. "Yeah?" Then he begins to smile, handing me the top of the glass, gingerly. "Where from? Radio Shack?"

I throw the glass in the garbage under the bar.

"I owe you one now, though," he says, glancing back over his shoulder. "How about if I molest her? And you can rescue her. Kung-fu me or something. We'll have to break something," he says, looking around. "Something else, I mean. Maybe that painting; never did—"

"Tony?"

He stops, looks at me.

"She's not the type."

"Modern, huh? I get it," he says. *"Moderne."*

He stands up, hesitates, then walks over to Glenna, all smiles. He sits on another of the low benches, on which he looks huge. I watch for a while then go back to washing glasses. On his way out Tony passes by the end of the bar and says, "I fixed it. The party. Gave it a little push."

Later, after the customers have cleared out, Glenna stops me by the back door when she's headed for her car and says, "You never said a word. I never even knew you were sick." And she smiles. Her eyes smile, there's sadness in them. I follow her out, through the store-room, two cases of beer bottles in my arms, trying to think of something to say.

She stops in the alley. "I'll cover my shift. Friday night'll be easy."

"Glenna—"

"Nine o'clock."

I'm leaning against the alley door. She walks away.

We arrive at the boat dock about ten and drive around looking for a place to park. I spot Tony's car, an old cream-colored Lincoln convert-ible with the top down. Cars are parked like pick-up-sticks. We add one.

There's a strong smell of diesel oil on the dock, where other people stand around waiting. No one I recognize. Someone says, "They pass by here every hour or so," and I'm ready to leave, but at this point the boat comes into view. It's big, brightly lit, with people hanging over railings on the two upper decks. The outside walls are painted in a pinkish white enamel; it glows. Glenna walks ahead of me, in jeans, and I wonder how I ever concluded she had no figure. The gangway leads to double doors into the big square main deck.

It's a great, smoky barn crowded with gaudy dancers. There's a teenage rock band, appropriately loud. The ceiling is low and there are scars in the floor where interior walls have been taken out. We bump into people. We dance.

While we dance, I notice, along one wall, the brown leather jacket and the moustache. I think I can smell the Gauloise, but decide that it's an illusion. Todd isn't an illusion; he's watching.

I catch Glenna in my arms and whisper to her, and she says, "Not now," and wheels around to look. Todd waves, points at her. "Son of a bitch," she says.

"I've got to find Tony anyway," I say. "Got to talk to him. I'll catch up with you."

A short blond woman in a leotard, shorts and leg warmers grabs Todd around the waist from behind. Glenna says, "Yeah, okay, I'll catch up with you."

I feel a strange hand at the back of my knee and look to see a woman pulling a child away, the kid's hand flailing in the air. When I turn back, Glenna's on her way.

I find Tony on the next deck up. There's no band, but the room is packed. Everyone seems to have a glass, all the glasses look like Old Fashioneds. They're serving everything in the same glass. Everyone is laughing.

A dark-skinned woman is sitting on the arm of the chair Tony's in; she's tall, looks Arabian. Two or three other people stand around him. When Tony sees me, he smiles.

"Her boyfriend is here," I say.

"Whose boyfriend?" Tony says, blinking. "What are you talking about?" He laughs as I crouch beside the chair. The others start to drift. "Settle down here, boy," Tony says. "Have a drink. Want to do some toot? Clear your head?" He leans forward. There's a big shell carved into the chair back.

"You invited Glenna's boyfriend. Do you remember last night? Glenna?"

"I remember," he says. "But look, I didn't invite anybody."

"This isn't your party?"

"Shit, no. Did you see all those Buicks, down by the dock? Would I know a lot of people with Buicks?"

"What did you tell her about me? That I was sick or something?"

"A small white lie; you caught me. You were never going to get it done. I just couldn't stand watching you pine over this emaciated—" He holds a hand up, as if to stop a blow "—but still breathtaking . . . schoolmarm." He shakes his head. "Don't worry, she didn't believe me."

"That's all you told her, that I was sick?"

"Well, maybe I told her you were sort of terminal." He laughs. In a solid black shirt, he looks like some kind of gigantic Jesuit. "You want a drink?" He waves at a waiter, and scoops two glasses off the tray when he comes near. "Here," Tony says. "Drink it straight down. You're magna uptight."

I take the drink and drink it down. It's bourbon, it burns.

"I tell you what," Tony says, looking around for the waiter again. "If you feel bad about it, I'll be happy to see that she gets home."

"You're getting married."

"In the morning," he says. "Ding-dong." He looks up over my head.

Two aggressively thin young men have stopped directly behind me, arguing. They have short hair, and both wear pin-striped vests over white shirts.

"I'm not the one who spent until four in the morning at Rudy's discussing lapis lazuli, for God's sake," one of them says. "How much can a person say about lapis lazuli, for God's sake?"

The other guy starts to say something, but the first one won't let him. "It's not even a real gemstone, for God's sake," he says. "It's just a rock."

Tony's looking at me. "I was just trying to help."

The angry guy turns to Tony, frowns. "Isn't that so?"

"For God's sake!" Tony says, nodding quickly.

I look up for the guy's reaction, but they're walking away, one following the other.

Tony's smiling. "See? They had thought love would solve all their problems." His expression turns serious. "Now you, you could have told her any time. You could have told her last night. Yet, here you are." The smile is very wide this time. "I was right," he says, standing up. "I was right."

He stumbles away. The people are all talking, fiercely, and I watch Tony nod, smile, and chuckle his way, looking for someone he knows, occasionally turning someone all the way around, until I can't see him any longer, and I sit in his chair and wave for a waiter.

It takes me a half-hour to find Glenna. She's outside, on the top deck in one of the metal chairs bolted to the wood, with her feet up on a railing. It's dark and quiet out here; I can hear the water slipping off the wheel and slapping the sides of the boat. The lights from houses scattered on the hillsides around the lake are distinct in the clear air. Sounds carry across the water.

"Hey," I shout, too loud.

Todd comes out of the darkness on the other side of her, looks at me, and says, "Hello, Guy."

"Hi, Todd."

"How's the liquor business, Guy?"

"It's good, Todd."

We go on like this, between long pauses, for about ten minutes. I try to remember the last time I have heard my name spoken twelve or fifteen times in ten minutes. Glenna doesn't say anything, just stares out over the water, smoking. I'm ready to pack it in.

Todd says, "Look, Guy, Glen and I were sort of trying to have a conversation, you know what I mean?" His tone's gotten snotty, and he's got one of those foul French cigarettes in his lips, kind of hanging. I check Glenna's cigarette but can't tell if it's the same brand.

We are gliding back to the dock, and in the growing light, staring at Todd, I see blood matted into his moustache, and his nose is sort of bent and there's blood there, too. I look from Glenna to him and back to her. Glenna doesn't understand, so I make a fist and point at her, asking. She nods, and I start laughing, can't help it.

"Look, Guy," Todd says, pushing against her legs, which are still hooked over the railing.

"Guy," Glenna says. "I'll meet you at the car in ten minutes."

On the dock, there seem to be as many people arriving as leaving. I stand and listen to car doors slam until Tony walks up with the Arab woman and introduces us. She speaks with a slight British accent.

Tony takes my arm and says, "I told her for you. Greta."

"Yeah, you told her for me."

"No, I mean I told her you weren't sick. Right after I talked to you. She laughed at me; she already knew. I told you she didn't believe me. Was that kid her boyfriend?" He's holding onto my arm with one hand, and the woman's arm with the other. "Hey, do you know what's phopho—" He turns to the woman.

"Phosphorylation," she says.

"Phosphorylation. She's a brain surgeon."

"I do research," she says.

"Phosphorylation is *very* interesting," Tony says, releasing my arm. "She hit him, did you know she hit him?" He feints toward my head with his massive forearm. "Blood all over the place. I'd watch myself." He gathers the woman and starts away, turns back to me and says, "The key to the whole thing is . . . equanimity. Okay?"

I stand on the driveway above the dock for another twenty minutes, watching people free their cars from the mess and drive away, and others arriving. Finally Glenna shows up, walking fast, finds me and stops, facing me like, I can't help thinking, a boxer.

"Guy," she says. "I quit. I don't have to give notice, do I? I quit. I don't work for you any more."

I just stare. She is very serious.

"I hit him. I expected it to be a pleasure. It wasn't. I felt sorry for him. That's all." She stops. "I need to get out of this mood. Can we go somewhere and talk?"

She is about five-eight and can't weigh much over 110. She has on a white vest-type thing that laces up the front, and her collarbone stands in high relief above it. I look at her long, thin, bare arms and I think, When you go to parties, you pay the price. If you go to parties, some dream or other is liable to come true.

"Well?"

I nod. "I can do that. I'd like to do that."

"I don't know what took you so long," she says, starting for the car.

"I was taking the mandatory eight count." She turns and looks, and I say, "Just a joke, Glenna."

"Not extremely funny," she says. There is a quick smile, and she says, "Okay. Somewhat funny." She looks unbearably fragile. So, probably, do I.

Stoner's Lament

It's just daylight. Stoner feels old and his legs are freezing. His pants legs feel too large, his jacket too thin. The service representative with the clipboard and the tie is tall, reminds him of his son, Andy, who used to come and work on cars in the garage, at the old house, before he divorced and moved to California, and Stoner retired and moved to the apartment. The car is old, too, he thinks. No point in spending ten thousand dollars on a new one you'd drive maybe a hundred miles a month, although he knows he is lying to himself. He doesn't drive a hundred miles a month, not even fifty; twenty is more like it, so there's no reason to buy a new one. He looks through the huge doors into the bays of the service department. All the cars are new, or newer, they don't have the chalky paint, they shine, small and silver. Toward the back there's a red one. His car is big and a milky blue, standing as if in dry-dock in the driveway behind him. When he drove up and pulled into the narrow lane beside the building, he jumped out of the car, jaunty, but something in the service representative's manner told him even before the kid said "These were great old cars" that he looked silly, trying to be jaunty. He told the kid he wanted tires, and the kid said, "Yep, you're ridin' on air there," and ran his soft, manicured fingers over the slick rubber on the right front. Now Stoner is thinking: Riding on air. It's cold.

"H 78-15, got some real balloons on this baby," the kid says, squatted down, reading the side of the tire. "Alignment's on special this week. You want us to align it?"

Stoner nods and says, "Sure. Go ahead. How much is that?"

The salesman stands to full height and pushes down on the fender with both hands, pulls his hands away like a dancer. The old Oldsmobile crackles a little. "Ought to lube it, too, while we're at it. Shocks?" He starts writing on the clipboard.

"Just the lube job," Stoner says. The shocks are new.

The kid looks down at him, gives a slight sigh. "The shocks control the car for you," he says. He looks again, waits, then shakes his head. "You want us to rotate 'em? No charge."

When Stoner asks for a written estimate, the kid says, "Wait a minute," then walks into the service area. Stoner watches him disappear through a steel door beside a big silver window which you can't see through. A guy in grimy red overalls brushes by and looks at Stoner's car, then gets in, like he owns it. He turns. "Where're the keys?"

The guy's hand, black with grease, grips the door, and his greasy fingers leave perfect prints behind on the chalky paint when he reaches for the key ring. He starts the car and jerks it into gear. "A real tanker, isn't it?" he says, pleasantly, and whips the car into the service area, taking it down out of sight to the opposite end.

The service rep comes out, accompanied by a wobbly man with a coat on and thinning hair. Stoner thinks, At least somebody here's over thirty. The new guy looks harried, but all smiles. "Mr. —" He looks at the clipboard. "—Stoner." The new guy holds out his hand. The young guy fades away.

"Is there some problem?" Stoner says, and looks down. "I asked for an estimate, that's all."

The wobbly guy says his name is Tom Thompson, laughs, says there's no problem. "Let's see," he says, "two tires, H 78-15. Big babies. Front-end alignment, lube job . . . " He writes on the form on the clipboard. "You're looking at about a hundred and seventy dollars, at the outside."

Stoner says nothing, reaches down to the pavement, picks up a short, dusty bolt and turns it in his fingers, slips it into the pocket of his jacket. His back hurts.

"Well, it'll probably come in ten or twenty dollars under that," the guy says, "but to be on the safe side . . . We have to write another ticket if I peg it too low." He holds the clipboard out. "Could I get your signature?"

Stoner signs and hands the clipboard and pen back. "You don't usually give estimates?"

Mr. Thompson laughs. "People don't ask for 'em much." He laughs again. "But I'm with you. I want an estimate. You can wait inside." He looks down the driveway, where two more of the little silver cars have pulled up, and guys with ties and clipboards are busy talking to the drivers. "Gonna be a long day," Thompson says.

The waiting room is actually two couches in broken brown Naugahyde and a big cannister ashtray in a tiny area opposite the parts department. Next to PARTS is SERVICE, another counter behind which two or three women sit talking across their desks. A corridor leads off to the showroom floor, Stoner can see the edges of a couple more of the shiny silver miniature cars, and behind them glass walls onto the street. There's a big white clock on the overhang above the parts counter. Eight fifteen in the morning. The couch is ugly but comfortable; Stoner's eyes start to close and he can feel his head fall forward, so he gets up and walks around into the corridor, following the smell of coffee. They want me to fall asleep, he thinks.

In the showroom, the cars' metallic paint sparkles with the sunlight coming through the glass walls. Stoner stares at the tires; they look tiny and ridiculous. He starts toward the nearest window sticker. "Sell you a car, Pop?" a voice says. This guy's clear-eyed and very relaxed, looks newborn in his corduroy sports coat. His face looks like the first one's hands, puffy and babyish. "Make you a good deal today on a Turbo." The guy's eyebrows flash up.

Stoner smiles. "Just a cup of coffee."

"Sure," the salesman says, and goes into one of the small offices off the showroom floor. He comes out and hands over the coffee, in a paper cup. "Make you a good trade on that old Buick," he says. He points out the side window, at the service lane. "I saw you."

"It's an Oldsmobile," Stoner says.

"About a '70?" the salesman says.

" '66." Stoner sips the coffee, which is lukewarm. "I don't drive enough to make it worth it to—"

"One of these babies, you could take it all the way to Florida," the kid says, watching a girl with white hair come through the front door of the showroom. "That turbo kicks in, you'd be flyin' down the freeway. The women'd be starin' at you." The kid laughs, slaps Stoner's shoulder, and turns away.

"Why are they all the same color?" Stoner says, but the kid is gone, headed for the girl with white hair, who's looking into one of the cars.

Stoner takes the bolt from his jacket pocket, looks at it, imagines a pile of bolts on the roof of one of the cars. Slipping it back in his pocket, he walks out. Back in the corridor, he looks at the women behind the service counter. One is reading. Another looks up, and he smiles, but she leans to one side, looking around him for the salesman back in the showroom. Stoner crumples the coffee cup, drops it in the ashtray, and sits back down on the brown couch. No one else waits in the waiting room. For a while he watches the guys behind the parts counter, as customers come in and joke with them while they punch away on computer terminals and talk about "snap rings" and "interlocks" and pins and springs and other words which are unrecognizable, and then, in spite of the coffee, he falls asleep.

He wakes up with Tom Thompson holding his shoulder. He hears voices, a woman saying, "Him! He was disposable. He was a real paper towel," and then there's laughter. Thompson looks worse than he did earlier, concerned, but that isn't it, he looks confused. "We have to get it from the warehouse and it'll take some time," Thompson says.

"House?" Stoner blinks, half awake. "Andy?" He shakes his head.

"Your tie-rod's bent," Thompson says, annoyed. "We have to replace it. Before we can align the front end. The car's so old we don't keep stock on it, but I called the warehouse and they said they have one. Just twenty bucks, and we can still do it today."

Abruptly the whole room becomes quiet. Stoner looks around Mr. Thompson. A young woman wearing brown overalls, white socks that say R E E B O K, a clip in her hair, walks up to the parts counter. She has to duck to talk to the clerk. She's about six four, and she slams something down on the counter. "I want a credit on this, Charlie," she says.

"You might want to take the courtesy car," Mr. Thompson says, looking away.

"You can't read, Shara?" the clerk says to the tall woman. He points to a sign on the wall. "See, it says, 'No returns on electrical parts.' That's because—"

"It's putting out direct current. You bench test these things before you sell 'em, Charlie? Or do you just sit there with your thumb—"

"Look, I'm gettin tired of you, Shara, you want to know the truth. You think you get some special treatment . . . just because you're some kind of freak?"

Stoner stands up. "Hey," he says, but Thompson is all over him. "If you'll just step outside, out there on the sidewalk, I think the courtesy-car driver just got back. I'll send him out to you." Thompson is pushing him toward the side door.

The woman and the clerk are staring at each other. "Don't bust anything, Shara, on your way out," the clerk says. "Truth is, we ain't paid up on our Kong policy."

The woman reaches across the parts counter. She has the clerk's shirt in one hand and the dirty cylinder she brought with her in the other. "The truth is, Charlie, you got two choices. Know what the second choice is? The second one is, Eat this alternator." She jerks his face toward it, holds him there. "I may be a freak, but I'm a freak that outweighs you forty pounds." She puts the alternator down gently on the counter, lets him go. "So . . . take the first choice."

Thompson has forgotten Stoner. "Shara, what's the trouble?"

The young woman turns around. Her light eyes are set in a stare. She brushes her hair away with her hand, leaving grease on her cheekbone. "No trouble, Tom. I just got this DC alternator here and I'd like a credit, and Charlie—" She looks back at the clerk. "We were discussing it." Above her eyes, eyeshadow, blue.

Thompson nods at the clerk, who looks back with a childish frown. Thompson nods again, and the clerk looks around, hopelessly, for someone to delegate the job to. The other parts clerks are all pretending to be busy, each with something in his hand, each staring down, smiling. "Charlie," Thompson says, "now." Then he remembers Stoner, and laughs, ushering him out through the door onto the sidewalk. "The courtesy car'll be right here. I'm sorry," he says.

"I'll walk."

"It's awfully cold," Thompson says. He blows into his cupped hands for emphasis, then reaches out. "You probably should let us—"

"I'll walk," Stoner says, shrugging off the man's hand.

"Okay." Thompson walks back inside, shaking his head.

When the young woman comes out, Stoner calls to her. "Did they give you your money?" he says, but she just looks at him, shivers, and walks over and gets up into a pickup. A shield painted on the door says 'Sharamotive'; a sticker on the back bumper says, white on black, VISUALIZE WORLD PEACE.

A few blocks from the dealership, the sidewalk becomes broad and faced with high-rise apartment buildings, not much different from Stoner's building across town. As he walks, he begins to inventory the junk on the sidewalk, on the street. Paper. Straws. A high-heeled shoe. Lock washer. Goes with the bolt, though it looks too small. He picks it up. He likes collecting things. People discard all sorts of things nowadays. Most of it you don't want to touch, but there's always something useful, he thinks, at least there's usually something; last week a dowel, a perfect piece of oak, three-eighths, lying in the gutter. So he walks, surveying this new territory.

Cigarette package, Winstons. A letter from *House and Garden.* Someone's glasses, not broken, nothing the matter with them. Bottles, cheap wine from the look of them. Not my part of town, Stoner thinks. Panties, white, cotton. He laughs.

When he sees three people approaching, Stoner tenses up a little, but as they draw closer, he sees their sweaters, matching gray, with reindeer in broad red bands across their chests. They're young, but they're not dangerous.

Up on the short strip of grass between the sidewalk and the wall, he sees something and stops. He looks twice. A rat, stiff, dead. It's been painted red with an inch-wide blue stripe down the center of its back. He looks again, to make sure. He pushes it with his shoe. It's too big to have been a pet, the thing's the size of a squirrel. Stoner looks up at the stone apartment building.

"Oh, I'm so sorry, Pops." The three young people are beside him, two men and a woman. "Was he a friend of yours?"

"C'mon," the woman says.

The first one, the talker, looks up at the building above them and says, "Suicide rat. Poor baby."

"C'mon," the woman says.

"I'm sorry, Pops," the talker says, putting his arm around Stoner's shoulders. Their breath is two clouds, side by side. "Had he been despondent for a long time? Months? Maybe this is just a cry for help," he says, grinning. He kicks at the painted rat. "Nope," he says.

Stoner pulls away, looks at the boy's sweater, then his eyes. He plants his feet wide on the sidewalk, and says, trying to drop his voice as low as he can, "Keep talking, son." His head is throbbing, his legs shake.

The kid in the reindeer sweater laughs, a quick little laugh. "Beg your pardon, maharaji?" He jerks his arm away from the woman, who is pulling at him.

"Two—" Stoner says, but he's already fouled it up. He doesn't blink. He tries to remember how it goes, but can't. All he can remember is eyeshadow. The third young person is already a hundred yards ahead. He hates his throbbing blood, his weak legs. But he doesn't blink. He says, "When you're through talking, you're going to eat that rat."

The kid looks at him. "You must be seventy years old."

"It's a disguise," Stoner says. He steps forward. "You through now?" He crouches down to the rat and picks it up; the body is rigid, but the fur, even with the paint, is soft. It's a cold thing but it's soft; he thinks of the hand with the paintbrush, the rat's teeth, biting, then he looks at the kid. "Yum," he says.

The kid looks to the side, then back at him. "You're old," he says, but his tone's gotten plaintive, babyish.

Stoner smiles and stands up, looks at the rat. He thinks, myocardial infarction; the smile twists on his face. He says, very slowly, very sweetly, "Keep talking."

"Come on," the woman says.

Reluctantly, looking back, the kid lets her drag him away. For half a block, until they reach an intersection, he looks back. Stoner, his hands shaking, sets the rat down where he found it, and closes his eyes.

When he turns and walks, the wind is sharp, but he smiles. As he walks, he imagines going to the bank and then back to the dealership with ten thousand dollars in bills in his jacket, walking in the showroom, and saying, "One of these silver babies." But then he thinks, in the spring, Andy will come from Santa Barbara, for a week or two, we'll buy rubbing compound, some wax, it'll give us something to do together, like at the old house, rubbing the dead chalky paint away, and then waxing the old car until it's blue again. He can almost see the car, shining, in its space in the parking garage under his apartment building. Visualize World Peace, he thinks, and looks around. It's cold, maybe it'll snow.

Liars

I pull out of the Townhouse parking lot, thinking about the cat, which has three legs. Three that work. A bag of beer and things with no preservatives, no caffeine, no sugar added on the brown back seat of the Rabbit. A six-pack of Diet Pepsi, which probably contains all the chemicals left out of the stuff in the bag.

There's a plump, pretty black girl standing on the sidewalk with her thumb up. It's a white neighborhood. I'm white. Five miles across the city, there are black sections. The city is small, still small enough to be divided this way.

Okay.

Getting in, she has a little trouble shutting the lightweight Volkswagen door, it doesn't latch automatically. She's not as plump as I thought, and she has sparkling eyes, hyped with eyeshadow which reflects the streetlights.

"Hi," the girl says, "where you going?"

While I'm getting up speed, phrasing an answer, she says, "You a ball player?" Blind siding me. I'm a market analyst, special opera tions, for Datatex. Mr. Math, my ex-wife used to call me. Secretly, I think I could've played defensive back in the N.F.L. Free safety.

"Yeah," I say.

The neat houses with their large, still green lawns look quiet, asleep. There's little traffic. It's fall, finally cooling off, and the cats are out. Every brick wall and parked Audi seems to have one.

"You got a smoke?" she says. "You a half back, I bet. I think I see you on TV on the Dallas Cowboys." She straightens herself on the seat, picking at one of her several layers of clothes. "My name's Peaches."

"Free safety," I say. "Defensive halfback."

I take my cigarettes from my shirt pocket, but she laughs and says, "I got one of those," then takes a pack of Marlboros from her purse, lights one and crumples the pack, tossing it onto the back seat with my groceries.

I make a turn, not toward my house but toward the other side of town. We pass a school where diehards are playing tennis under lights on courts at one corner of the grounds. I played there once with a woman who arrived with two kids in a silver Seville. A Donnay racket and passing shots which kept me spinning around like an animal. Afterward the woman said, "You play quite well; aggressively," took the children and drove off.

"Well, looky there," Peaches says, watching the tennis players. "That's sure enough Steely Swede, playin' tennis. Practicing up. Must be there's a big tournament. You know him?"

"Who's that?"

"Steely Swede," she says. "Born Borg." She has this exaggeratedly puzzled look on her pretty, child's face.

"Oh, yeah," I say, "but not really. Just to say hello to, you know."

I look back at the road just in time to see a yellow Mercedes full of blond women which has turned out from a side street. I hit the brakes, and when the woman driving hears my tires squeal, she brakes too, so that I have to jerk the Rabbit into the other lane to avoid hitting them. As we whip past the Mercedes, Peaches leans out and yells, "Sick hunky bitch!" and waves her fist.

She turns back to me. "You drive real good, half back," she says. "I was wonderin'. You get me a date with Born Borg?"

"He's married," I say.

"We all married," she says.

"I don't think he's got a phone."

"Never mind, half back. Born Borg probably got a little short girlie be wonderin' why he don't call her up. And I got this date with you, anyhow. We could play tennis, you got your racket?" She's looking around into the back seat. "My Daddy's got brand new tennis courts."

"I got this bad leg," I say. "An accident. I'd like to, but I got this bum leg."

Peaches is wearing a blue denim jumpsuit over an old sweatshirt. She's tugging at the open zipper running down the front of the jumpsuit. It's broken. "Damn Lionel," she says. "Done tore my suit I just bought."

"How about if I drop you downtown?" I say. "You know your way from downtown?"

But she doesn't say anything, she's still working on the zipper. We stop at a light. Her features are round, soft. She's seventeen or eighteen. She's a kid.

"Half back, I do truly know what that look means," she says. "You married, aren't you?" The light changes, and the woman in the yellow Mercedes leans on her horn. Peaches looks back, then says, "Can you just hol' this here?" yanking one side of the zipper out toward me. I gun the engine and the Rabbit sputters away from the intersection.

"Divorced," I say.

She's flicking ashes on the floor. I pull the ashtray out from the center dash, a metallic shriek. She punches buttons on the radio, which is lit up, but doesn't work. "What's the matter with it?"

"It's broken."

"Oh," she says, staring at a young cop who has pulled up beside us at the next stoplight. The cop has a shotgun upright in the middle of the front seat. He's real sexy, in a country sort of way.

"Peaches," I say, and she turns back. The cop is smiling. He pulls away as the light changes. There are three cars behind us and we all crawl down the street in formation behind the cop, like at a race when the caution flag is out, for an accident. The cop drives slower and slower. After three or four blocks, he turns off.

"Peaches isn't really my name," she says. "It's Jacqueline. I just tol' you that till I knew you were safe."

She opens and closes the glove compartment, runs a hand over the black vinyl on the top of the dash. "Sure a nice car you got. This a foreign car isn't it? Gonna get me a foreign car." She turns toward me, both hands on my arm. "You can get me a date with that Tony, uh— Tony Dor-*sett?*" She stresses the last syllable of the name, proudly.

"Fact is, Jacqueline—"

"Call me Peaches," she says. "I got one of them Trans-Am now. I just metal the pedal, ain't nobody can catch me. Rrooom."

We stop at another light and we're surrounded by yellow cars. The Mercedes is beside us. The four women are laughing, shooting the finger, talking to us, but their windows are all up. Behind us, a yellow Corolla. Something else, yellow, makes a squealing left turn across in front of us. All the cars are occupied by white women. All the women have permanents, it's a freak show of tight, tiny curls.

"I'll just drop you up ahead here, I gotta get this stuff to a refrigerator." I wave toward the groceries in the back seat.

Peaches doesn't like this at all. She's looking around as if at Hong Kong.

"I'm afraid," she says, frowning. "I'll go to Six Street. Damn Lionel. Just off and left me. He said we was gone to dinner, but we wasn't. He wanted me for lunch. I said, No dinner, no lunch. You could take me on down there. You're nice." She's not getting out of the car. She starts after the zipper on the jumpsuit again, but gives up. "Lionel lied to me, that's all."

On the edge of downtown there are old houses converted to offices, lawyers mostly. After a couple more blocks, Peaches is patting my arm and pointing. There's a gaunt white kid standing next to a mailbox. He has bushy red hair and looks like he hasn't eaten for a week. I pretend not to see him but Peaches won't have it. "Maybe he's got some smoke," she says.

After I've already stopped the car, the kid remembers and throws his hand out, thumb up. He gathers something off the top of the mailbox and slides into the back seat.

"Far out," the kid says. He's wearing one of those sweatshirt parkas. His eyes are bright blue, they don't blink, and they seem to have a sort of glaze over them. He talks very fast. When Peaches asks if he has any dope, he fumbles in a pocket and produces a joint in wrinkled gold paper. He straightens it out and he and Peaches share it.

Downtown is small, maybe twenty square blocks. We cross Texas Avenue, which is really main street, empty at night, with the city's half-dozen reflective glass buildings all lined up in a tiny mockery of Houston. Past Texas, everything drops back to two stories and, as if in a cartoon, the population changes color. There's a liquor store. Peaches wants to stop. Cigarettes.

She gets out of the Rabbit and goes inside. A couple guys duded out in hats, capes, scarves, turn in after her.

At the curb I leave the engine running quietly and slump back against the door, looking into the bright store. The red-haired kid says his name is Rex. He puts my bag of groceries, which by now is soaked through and ripped, on the floor, and sits on the edge of the seat.

"This your car?" he says. "She your old lady?"

"No."

"Your car?" he says again. "My name's Rex, named after Rex Harris, some actor, you know. She's black. Not your old lady then you won't wheeze if we got together. You know, black chicks have the hardest time of all." He does a sort of cough, and then swallows three or four times, quickly, then coughs again. His throat is sunken, reddish, over a narrow collarbone. "Boy, sure would like a beer," he says, looking around. "Goddamn!" He's looking at the store.

Inside, the two dudes are dancing in close to Peaches, then away, laughing, one with his arm around her, then the other. The owner, also black, handsome, balding, in a black on white plaid shirt, looks like he hates them.

Rex has the back door of the car open, and he looks at me. "Aren't you coming?" he says.

"Slow down, Rex. Let's think it over."

"Shit," he says.

"Look, I was just going to the grocery store. She can probably handle it."

"You big guys are all alike," he says. "Got rubber guts. Jesus." Still he doesn't seem overeager to rescue her by himself. He shoves his hand down into a pocket and comes up with a pill, a black capsule.

"What's that?"

"What's it to you?" he says, and heads into the store.

Inside, Peaches and one of the guys, the tall one, have partially disappeared behind a rack of wine. The other guy is carting bottles, one at a time, to the checkout counter, setting each down with a flourish. Then he goes back to the shelves and makes an elaborate show of deciding on the next bottle. Playing.

I think about just driving home, but before long it's clear that Rex has got things completely out of control. I shut off the engine and follow him inside.

"This your big gun?" the little dude, the one who was collecting bottles, says. He's wearing a cape over an iridescent green shirt. The tall guy with Peaches is in a big black frock coat. As they come around the wine rack he takes something out of the pocket, a razor. He flips it open. I couldn't tell from the car—he's white. *White*, I think.

"It's Rubber Sally," Rex says. The guy in the cape has him up against the glass doors of a refrigerator. "Hey, blood," Rex says to him, "why don't we all— Hey." The guy is standing on Rex's foot.

"Who you callin' blood?" he says. "I show you some blood." The tall one starts for me. "Billy," the first dude calls to him, "boy here wants to see some blood, you got any blood?"

"Fresh out," Billy says. "Got no blood of y'own?" He's real loose. The razor's swinging from his left hand. Mother-of-pearl.

The little guy shakes his head. "Wonder if Red Ridin' Hood here got any blood?"

Rex's face twists up as the guy crushes his running shoe with a boot heel. Billy is breathing on me now. A big nose, long, delicate black moustache, pockmarks in his skin.

"Other hand," he says, "this one here look like he got no mo' blood'n a toad. Correct?"

"What we do is check," the little guy says. "That's what the CIA do. We check, in a situation like this one we got here."

"Correct," Billy says.

I look around for the store owner, who is sitting on a barstool behind the counter, watching. He just stares at me. There's a telephone on the counter in front of him, next to the bottles the little guy was collecting.

"Now you leave him alone now," Peaches says. "He's on the Dallas Cowboys."

"That a fact, Sally?" the guy on Rex says. "What you doing on the Dallas Cowboys named Sally? He on the Dallas Cowboys, too?" he says, waving a hand toward Rex.

My head is pounding. "Tony Dorsett," I say. I take a step backward, to get out of Billy's breath. "That's Tony Dorsett, didn't you recognize him?"

"No shit?" the guy says, taking a closer look at Rex. "Look a little red to be Tony Dorsett."

"Well we shoot him up, before the games I mean. Chemicals, you know."

"Little chemotherapy? Then he turn black?"

"Yeah," I say. "Sure."

"Hey, Judge," Billy says, "you heard. Let that bro up. De-foot. You busting toes on the world's fastest human."

Judge lets Rex go, and Rex heads for the door.

"We can go now?" I say.

Judge, holding his cape, sweeps his arm toward the door. Rex has already limped out onto the sidewalk. The owner motions for Billy to come to the counter but he ignores him. "You stayin' or goin', Mama?" Billy says.

Peaches looks at me, then at him.

Billy smiles wide, slides his arm around her, and says, "Sure, Mama, I buy you the biggest bottle in the house."

When I get on the sidewalk, I can barely breathe and the lights are bright and smeared. Rex is in the Rabbit with a can of beer. He hands me one as I get back behind the wheel.

"You want a beer?" he says. "Sorta hot."

I put the key in and just sit for a second, close my eyes, with the beer sweating in my hand.

"Jesus," he says, "I thought we were dead meat, there for a second."

"Rex?"

"Yeah?"

"I really like you."

"Say what?" he says.

"Get out of my car."

He blinks now, several times, like he doesn't quite understand, but he gets out and starts away down the sidewalk. After I pass him, I hear him yell something, he calls me a name.

Zach

Whenever Zach went out with the new girl and came home late, the cat got mad, stalked around the house like Patton, its long banded tail whipping back and forth in the early morning light.

It was after the woman left with her suitcases. She walked down to the corner so Zach didn't have to see the guy's car, her idea of thoughtful. He had wanted to see the car. Some car to imagine her in; laughing, probably. Poor son of a bitch, he thought. She never laughs.

The cat put gray, black and white cat hairs on Zach's shirts and, sometimes, in his eyes. The cat was no match for the woman when it came to telling him what was wrong with him, how he was a bad guy. The woman was a virtuoso. The cat couldn't talk. What a blessing.

A few weeks later, the woman's new boyfriend, Benner, came with a truck, to pick up her things. Benner the enlightened sort. A frowner, very serious. Not a bad guy, Zach thought. Poor son of a bitch, he thought.

"Never known anyone like her," Benner said. "She wanted the salt shakers."

Zach pointed to the kitchen. "In there," he said. "Far right-hand drawer. I figured she'd want them."

Benner gathered her things. His shyness, as he walked through the small house, was appealing. Zach had already put most of it in cardboard boxes, by the door.

Sometimes she laughs, Zach thought. She laughed when I said, "You're aces." Again when I said, "I got that out of a Clark Gable movie." But later, when there was no money, she didn't laugh. She'd stand out back and play like she was watering plants and wish she was somewhere else. If she hadn't been out there, I would have.

Zach closed his eyes and tried to tell what the house smelled like, but couldn't.

Benner needed help with the heavy stuff. A table and some chairs. A dinette from her grandmother's house, old and heavy. And the TV, the color.

"Damn," Zach said, standing in the street with Benner, looking at the dinette in the back of the truck.

"I'm sorry about all this," Benner said.

They walked back up the driveway and into the house and he gave Benner iced tea. "You want a beer?" Zach said.

"Tea's fine." There was sweat on Benner's forehead, four or five drops in an impossibly straight line. "She wanted me to bring the cat."

"I told her I'd think about it." Zach looked around the living room. "That's all I told her."

"You want to keep the cat," Benner said, thinking it over, nodding. "My ex-wife kept my cat, my second one. She boarded it and it got some kind of respiratory thing, and something else, and then they gave it the wrong anesthetic. Killed it. You know, nobody knows what they're doing." Benner stood up, frowned, wiped his forehead with his sleeve. "She'll probably call you."

The girl Zach met was twenty-two. Her name was Suzanne. A long, thin nose, bright eyes, no eyebrows to speak of. More handsome than beautiful, but beautiful, too, he thought, how can anyone who's twenty-two be anything but beautiful? She worked for a dentist and went to school.

"What's your major, isn't that what I'm supposed to say?"

They went to movies and bars. Later he took her home and introduced her to the cat, sent out for pizza, watched television. When you have money, you send out for pizza, Zach thought, and she asked him what he was thinking, and he told her.

"And go to shopping malls," she said.

"And buy pink shirts you never wear."

"You bought a pink shirt?"

"It's all right, isn't it?" Zach said. "I used to look at that shirt, when I didn't have any money, and think, Twenty-seven fifty, My God."

"I took back a bottle of perfume, once. I mean, three years after I bought it. Put water in it," she said. "Then I stole a bottle of perfume and sold that back."

He nodded, but must have looked at her funny, because she said, "It was a one-time thing, I'm not in the habit."

"Lucky not to get caught," Zach said.

"The guy I was living with went with me. He flirted with the salesgirl. It was all planned out, like we were doing a Brinks job. He was very careful about everything. Planned it out."

Zach thought, She used to live with Benner.

She looked at him, put down her pizza. "The really scary thing was selling it back. It was a one-time thing. I was petrified." She was nervous. "Are you okay?"

"Suzanne," he said.

Later, he lay in jeans and no shirt on the bed, looking into the cat's gray-green eyes. Suzanne sat beside him, rubbing his back.

"Don't try and outstare a cat," he said. "They attack. They really don't like it." He wondered if it was true, this thing he had been told.

"I don't believe that," Suzanne said.

She was kneading his skin at the shoulders and when she pinched his neck too hard he jumped. "Damn, Lynn!"

Suzanne drew her hands away, he could feel them floating in the air above his back. The cat settled itself, rocking gently on the bedspread.

"I'm sorry," he said. "It'll happen to you. Somebody gets into your mind, and it takes a while to get them out. It takes a while," he said. "Not too long."

"Zach," she said, "it's happened to me. I'm not a kid."

"There's nothing the matter with being a kid," he said, waiting for her hands.

He was at work when they took the cat. He got home at six, and looked for the cat. He used to get home and look for the woman. Now, the cat. He checked the window sills, pulling curtains aside, the gray shelves in the bathroom closet where the cat was hard to see, and the filthy space behind the stove. Opened kitchen cabinets and looked in with a flashlight, even the cabinets the cat couldn't open, the ones with strong catches. He thought, Don't panic.

New places. The hole in the records where the female vocalists had been. The empty space in the suitcases. The black director's chairs, which looked stupid pushed up under the table Suzanne had picked out at a yard sale.

He called the woman, got no answer, and a half-hour later, tried again.

"You're accusing me of stealing a cat?" she said. "Which is, incidentally, my own cat."

"You got the good car, the good television, I even gave you the pliers. Taking the cat seems a little greedy."

"Zach," she said, "I don't have the cat. And I don't have to take care of you any more. I'll leave the pliers on the porch here for you."

He heard the woman, who had never really mastered covering the phone, say "No!" and then something else he couldn't make out. She came back.

"Did you look on the gray shelves in the bathroom?" she said. He didn't answer. "Never mind," she said. "When you find him, though, he belongs to me."

"You're real good at this. Lying, I mean."

"We all have our faults," she said, and hung up.

He went back and looked in the bathroom closet, then sat in the bedroom with the other telephone and called Suzanne, until she answered at one.

Suzanne said, "Don't panic," and then, "I can't believe I said that," and then she laughed. "Cats always come home," she said. "Do you want to meet me somewhere? Do you want me to come over?"

"You think I'm crazy," he said.

"I think it'll work out."

She came over. She fell asleep, curled at one end of the couch in the living room. Zach put a blanket over her.

In the morning they went to work. Later, he took her to dinner at a new place, with racquetball rackets and sports shoes on the walls, a sports motif. The food was good, and expensive.

"Shish kebab is not sporty food," she said. "Not really."

"The rice," he said, lifting some with his fork. "You're supposed to notice the funny rice."

She nodded. "Lots of vegetables, on the menu."

He talked about the woman, after apologizing for it, on the drive back to his house, and in the living room, with the TV going, the little one, black and white. They sat together on the couch with the window to the lawn and street behind them.

It was twelve-thirty in the morning when the truck pulled up outside. Zach didn't hear it stop but he heard the big heavy door slam on the street, and thought, Pickup, and turned his head.

It was almost cold outside and the person coming stepped crisply up the walk with his arms folded over his chest, at least it looked that way in the dim light from the streetlights, over the near hedge. Benner knocked on the door.

The cat seemed to like him. "Benner," Zach said, taking the cat, "this is Suzanne. You want a beer? You look like hell."

Benner nodded, sitting on the edge of an end table, in a corduroy coat.

Zach carried the cat into the kitchen, set it down in front of the refrigerator. It ran back toward the living room, sniffing. Zach got out three beers and listened for Suzanne's voice, but they weren't talking.

"I'm sorry about all this," Benner said, when Zach got back and sat down next to the cat. "It was her idea, bringing him back, I mean. She knew she'd made a mistake."

"It's all right," Zach said. "Much her cat as mine, probably."

"We had a little argument about it."

"There's no such thing as a little argument with Lynn."

Benner smiled. "Boy, that's the truth," he said, setting the beer can down precisely in the ring of condensation it had left on the table. "But she comes around."

"Yeah," Zach said, "she comes around." He shrugged. "Cigarette?"

"I don't smoke," Benner said, taking another drink, and setting the can back down. He looked around the living room. "I've gotta go."

After the truck was gone, Zach talked, apologizing first, then listing off for Suzanne the woman's good qualities, as well as he could remember them, including some he made up out of nothing, until he thought the list was long enough, then he apologized again, and said, "Can we talk about something else?"

Suzanne said, "He's too clean. He looks like a robot."

"Benner? He's not a bad guy."

"No, he was a nice guy. But his shirt looked like it buttoned at the crotch or something."

"He's not a bad guy," Zach said. "He's probably good for her or something."

She looked at him.

He took her wrist, turned it so he could see her watch, upside down. He stood up, brushed his sleeves and the front of his shirt. "One o'clock," he said. "Let's you and me go out and look for a good, dark bar. There's still an hour."

"Okay," Suzanne said.

"Okay."

Failing All Else

Failing all else, he read a story about falling in love.

"Want to hear this story?" he said.

"Huh?"

"I said, Do you want to hear this story?"

"Sure, why not, okay?" She nodded. She looked at her watch, a Seiko, dabbed at a gob of something on the tablecloth with her finger. "How long is it?"

He looked at her across the table, on which there were two bowls of double-chocolate ice cream, brownies, an eclair.

She looked out the tall glass windows of the cafe.

He said,

He was tall and walked with a limp. Once when he was younger, but not really young, he lived in Denver, a city in Colorado, and in that city had been walking along the levee, past a huge brown barge loaded—

"There's no levee in Denver," she said.

Those are not brownie crumbs, he thought, staring at her lips. She must have sneaked a piece of cake. She noticed him staring.

"Okay, okay," she said. "So he was walking along this nonexistent levee. Then what?"

he was walking past a huge, red-brown barge tied up at the levee, loaded high with barrels of gold.

"Wait a minute."

"What now?" he said. She *had* sneaked a piece of cake, the plate obscured from his view by the salt and pepper shakers, huge white ceramic ones in the shape of children, a boy and a girl. The children were surprisingly ugly.

"I need a napkin," she said, standing up. She went for it at the counter where the sign said, TRY OUR WHOLE-WHEAT BUN, came back and sat down. He watched her look at her watch.

He continued,

Toward the front of the barge, for it was enormous, and carried many different cargoes, were the steel bars of a thousand cages. In each cage, a bear. Some brown bears, some black bears, sloth bears, sun bears, and, in the last cage, a pure white bear. A short, pure white bear. A funny-looking short pure white bear, which didn't growl like a bear, or stand like a bear, or, when he got close, even look like a bear. The white fur reminded him of rabbit fur, with which he was familiar, having once herded rabbits up the Chisholm Trail with John Wayne and—

"You're making this up," she said. "Let me see that."

He jerked the book up, away from the table, thankful that she had interrupted at just that point, because he had momentarily forgotten who was on the trail ride.

and Montgomery Cliff, also Harry Carey, Walter Brennan and John Ireland—

"That's Clift," she said.

and John Clift. Anyway, this bear's fur looked like that of a white rabbit, a sort of fur he knew well from his rabbit-punching days. "Hey," he cried, gripping the blue steel bars, "that's the sorriest excuse for a bear suit I ever saw. If that's not a man in a bear suit, I'm Marco Polo," which was not entirely correct, because the party who stepped out of the bear suit was a woman, of course the most beautiful woman he had ever seen. She had yellow hair and soaring cheekbones and the rest, and because she was also naked, he could observe that the rest of her was choice as well, given a final, fitting touch of perfection by the fact that her right breast, the larger, pointed toward Wichita, Kansas. No matter which way she turned, the breast honed in on Wichita. "What's so special about Wichita?" he said, to which the woman replied, lowering her stunning lids over her striking eyes and with sort of a smile, "The man I love loved me in Wichita."

"Will this story get really real pretty soon," the girl said, signaling for the waitress, for another bowl of double-chocolate. The waitress was impossibly tall. Also dark and handsome, and Finnish; he had asked once.

"Really real?" he said.

"You know," she said. She smirked. She was not tall, but she was wearing a gold shirred-front Kamali bathing suit and a black felt skirt. She had beautiful shoulders. Toothsome was the word which came into his mind, briefly. I'm hopeless, he thought, Jesus, toothsome.

"Well, he's got to get her out of the bear cage, first," he said.

"No, he doesn't," she said, grinning. It was sort of a grin. "They could . . . "

Jesu Christi, he thought.

Just about this time the captain of the tugboat, which was tied up to the levee upstream of the barge, came wandering down the dock and offered the limping man a job unloading the barrels of gold. "What's with all these bears?" the man said; "Some kind of circus?" The skipper looked at the sagging bears in a kindly sort of way, laughed. "Yeah, you could say that. They're dancing bears. Do you want the job, or not?" "Yeah, okay," the man said, and set to unloading the large round ribbed barrels, setting them along the dock. Mon Dieu, he thought, they could've used smaller barrels; somebody should have told them about gold. He took his shirt off. After a couple hours he climbed onto the barge and lay back in the rust and dust. The woman got back out of her bear suit and watched him sweat where he lay on the deck. The bears watched, too, slumped over in their chairs, with sad eyes. "They really keep you in a cage?" he said, without turning his head, staring straight up into the crimson Colorado sky. "They?" she said; "there's no they." He looked at her. She pointed to the cage's dressing and vanity area where he saw, hung over the mirror on a strip of leather, a key by Tellingham Co., Ltd, London, which he recognized only by virtue of his long acquaintance with Basil Rathbone. "Then why don't you escape?" he said, which made the most beautiful woman angry. "Escape what? It's warm in here, at least it was when the man I love loved me, which he probably still does, because he is of course perfect. If you follow me. And then there're the three impossible things. Only the man I love knows the trick of the three impossible things, I think." "Mea maxima culpa," he said, "forget I mentioned it. Gotta go. I only get fifteen minutes for my break," he said, limping away for more barrels. By nightfall he had maybe fifty barrels on the dock. Another ten thousand or so were still on the barge when he climbed aboard to sleep. In his dream he wondered, The three impossible things? and the most beautiful woman heard him wondering because among her many other splendid traits she could of course slip in and out of dreams at will—

"A dream lover," the girl said, unwrapping a Three Musketeers bar. She held it up. "Keep them in the freezer, drop them in my purse, so when I'm ready, they're ready."

"What?" he said. He was looking at the highlights from the gold leotard, tracking the sunlight which bounced into the cafe from the side windows of cars on the street.

"This woman's a dream," she said.

"Yeah, right, sort of," he said. He heard, distant, light, Scandinavian, the waitress's laughter. He continued,

and the most beautiful woman, who now watched him sleep, slipped in and out of his dream, at will, and explained the three impossible things. "The first impossible thing," she said, "is to bring me a barrel of gold." That's easy, he thought, and in his dream, hopped off the barge onto the dock. "A new one," she said. Jesu Christi, he thought. But he set to it anyway, picking up an empty barrel in Irkutsk, filling it to overflowing at an outlying goldspring, at night, and while rolling the barrel all the way from the Soviet Union was hard work, especially when he had to convince the border people, by smearing the outside of the barrel with sturgeon and carrying the gold in his shoe in several trips back and forth, even more amazing when one recalls that what he was shuffling across was the Bering Strait, this done, it became clear that the first impossible thing was not impossible at all. Although it was tiring. When he got back he smiled at her, through the bars, and said, "Where do you want the gold, lady?" and the barrel slipped from his hands and fell on his foot, leaving him with some fractured bones (there being so many in the foot that repair is nearly impossible and considered frivolous). Luckily, it was the same foot, which gave him only a slightly more pronounced limp, and in any case he was so happy at having proved the first impossible thing possible, and having accomplished it, that he scarcely noticed the blood. What, he thought, is the second thing? "It's harder than it looks," she said. What is it? he thought, Just give me the assignment. "Okay, smart aleck," she said. "The second impossible thing is to fill my life with dancing bears." This set him to thinking. "New ones," she said, but he had assumed that. He gazed over the mass of cages and barrels on the barge, in his dream, and saw the bears he would bring, lined up beside the others. He thought, Why do we do it? But this lapse into better judgment lasted only until he could formulate his next thought, which was, This bitch thinks she's seen some dancing bears; I'll show her some dancing bears! and he set off. After wandering six weeks he limped into park headquarters, sat on a redwood table and thought, Where can they be hiding? So he took a train to Wichita, Kansas, where he found the man who loved her sitting by the tracks. "What's the story on these bears?" he said. The Kansas man laughed. "Goddamn woman comes and looks at you and says to herself, you can see her saying it, this sorry slob could never fill my life with dancing bears tra-la, woman into whose life you could fit maybe ten or fifteen dancing bears with a shoehorn and a bear-shrinker, woman who wouldn't know a dancing bear from an Oldsmobile; I have dug ditches and unloaded bricks, you know, with brick tongs, eight bricks at a time, all afternoon, from a truck, but the hardest work I ever did was filling lives with dancing bears." "Yes, yes, but where did you find them?" The Kansas man looked at him and shook his head. "Well, I tell you, I get mine out of the bible." "The Bible?" "Not that Bible, any bible will do," the Kansas man said, walking away down the gravel roadbed, the two men limping in opposite directions now. The man stopped, after he had gotten fifteen or twenty yards, and shouted back, "Watch them. You gotta be quick. Bible bears wear out real fast. Not real dancers, either, I think sometimes." This wasn't much help. He looked down at his bible, in his hand. One goddamn page, he thought, I should've kept the rest of it. Still, in his dream, he

*tried, staring at the handwritten page with alacrity, and there emerged
certain small, slightly weird but it seemed to him durable bears who, on
the train to Colorado in the aisles between the dirty seats, picking up peanuts and scraps of foil, not pausing for sleep and wholly indifferent to his
commands, all the way down to the docks and up on to the deck of the
barge, danced.* "Ha!" *he cried, standing beside her.*

"Ha?" the girl said, swallowing, with an eclair in each hand.

"It's something they used to say in stories," he said. Goddamn, he
thought, I'm hungry. "This is an old story," he said.

The waitress came and took away the ice cream bowls, plates and
the glass the sundae had been served in. Name is Elga or something,
he thought, watching her fade away in the long delicate dress. He
remembered meeting the girl the first time, on some steps, in a dress.

"I think I read this story," the girl said. "He gets some in the end,
right?"

"You never read this story."

*Anyway, to make a long story short, he was quite pleased with himself
now, maybe too pleased, because this "Ha!" brought up the third impossible
thing, which, with great relish, great coyness, a hint of meanness, the ad-
mittedly wonderful and clearly most beautiful woman reminded him of,
and, at length, after shucking and jiving for what seemed a very long
time, told him. What is the third thing? he thought, and she, in his
dream, said, "It's simple, like most really impossible things," not being
able to resist this bit of whatever it was, "the third impossible thing is to
care less for me than I care for you."*
*He sat on a barrel on the barge in the freezing night air and thought about
this third thing for a long time, so long that he could no more feel the cold
which means it was the closest thing to forever because the one thing he
could feel if it was anywhere in the vicinity, whether he was awake or
asleep, even after he was dead, was the cold, after brooding that long, he
thought, All that work for nothing. He thought, Yes, that's true, I can't
do it. If I try to fake it, she'll see through it. Maybe not. Maybe one of
these dumb bears wants to go to a movie. Get one to slow down. And the
woman, bright-eyed and most beautiful, reaching for the key from the mirror, said, "But, in your case, I'll make another—"*

"Look at what time it is," the girl said, looking at her watch once
more, and though it wasn't really late, she started gathering her

things. "That's a really swell story. The eclairs aren't *perfecto,* but God they're sweet, you want this?" Pushing the last of the last eclair toward him on the table.

He limped after her, to the door, watched her disappear down the sidewalk, then went back to the table where he dropped two bills, a ten and a five, and the waitress accidentally stepped on the side of his foot and then apologized, saying, "I'm really sorry," and "What's that book you're reading?"

"You read it to me," he said, and handed her the book, and they sat down together.

Michael

In the small, bright room Michael's animals stand on all the window sills, on his desk, and over his head on a long shelf. There are wooden turtles, spiders, dinosaurs, even a cat or two, but mostly it's snakes, some curling, some coiled, some, improbably, standing straight up in the air. They are cut from many different woods, more shades of brown than I knew existed. Michael is on the telephone, talking about money.

The animals are two-dimensional, profiles really, but by shallow cuts and curves and using the patterns in the woods, he has gotten three dimensions out of two.

"This is walnut," I say, pointing to a small, heavyset tortoise. Michael nods, hanging up the phone. The wood is unfinished, there's a tiny hint of blue in it.

"I tried to make some turtles without that grin," he says, "just fooling around. Forget it. People think turtles grin *all the time*."

Michael is fat, has always been fat, except for a year or so in the early days of his business, when it was going well. He went on a diet and lost forty pounds. When I saw him I thought he was sick. Now the business is going under and he's fat again, balding a little but his hair's still sloppy, clear blue eyes. Looking at him, I remember that we are no longer children.

The room is his office, a glassed-in former garage. Outside, beyond the truck we came back from the airport in, thousands of pine trees are split by the highway wandering up and down the hills.

"Isn't that great stuff?" he says, noticing me looking at one of the acrobatic snakes which is made of a very dark wood. "It's called purple heart." He yawns and rubs his sweatshirt, both hands on his belly. "I want you in Austin with me tomorrow; nice sane corporate type like yourself, maybe you can persuade Mark to give me this loan."

"He's *your* brother."

"Yeah, but it's not his bank. I've been hoping for years, you know, that he'd start his own." He stands up. "Show you my shop."

Michael ducks his head to clear the low doorway into the house, and I follow him. In the house, too, there are wooden animals, but no snakes. Cats, elephants, a dozen poodle-sized ants. A fat VTOL airplane, plywood with an oak or ash veneer, stands in the front hall.

Michael's shop is a long patio, enclosed now, at the opposite end of the house from the office. The rough, red tile floor is covered with sawdust from table, band, and jig saws, a small lathe, drills, sanders. Outside, behind the house, there's a portable building where he finishes things. Packing crates with M E X I C O or K O R E A stenciled on in black are piled along one wall.

"Get them from an import joint," Michael says. "It's cheaper than building them." He closes the door to the shop and leads me back to the kitchen.

When I ask why there are no snakes in the house, the living quarters, Michael laughs. "Arthur. Arthur was afraid of snakes. He did one of my brochures, actually what you'd call a flyer, a little thing, and he printed the damn snakes upside down." He looks around the kitchen. "Guess I could move 'em in now."

"Where is Arthur?"

"Down in Houston. Poor Arthur." Michael is smiling. "He's a tart, really. Think I'll try another woman. Women are all right, don't you think?"

He gets up and brings a pair of scissors and a magazine from the living room. He flips it open and in less than a minute holds up his woman, a young Polynesian girl in a bathing suit with a big rectangular briefcase hanging from one hand. In the ad, the briefcase was part of a beach. "I think they're all right," he says. "Women. I'll ask Susanna. She's my expert."

"See her tomorrow in town?" I say.

"Yeah." He hands the paper doll to me. "You keep her," he says. "A fine woman like this wouldn't go for a bankrupt fat boy." He starts cutting in the leftover paper, but stops, crumples it and hooks it over my head into a grocery sack beside the refrigerator. "Doctor J," he says. His big face turns serious. "I think I'd rather have a cat. Couldn't have a cat. Arthur was allergic."

Dinner consists of wild rice topped with stringy meat which is surprisingly tasty until Michael tells me what it is. "Squirrel," he says, "I get it from the locals. They eat everything around here."

After dinner he asks me to look over what he calls his "books," three handmade gray ledgers with everything entered in a precise, priestly hand.

"You don't understand," I say, "I can barely balance my checkbook."

"C'mon. Got to be ready for Mark."

"Michael, everybody with a pension plan looks the same to you. You're a bigot."

"I know, I know, but so's Mark. Only he's your kind of bigot." He laughs.

He washes dishes while I look through the gray books, feeling uncomfortable. He sells wooden animals all over the country. The totals along the bottoms of the pages are surprisingly large, but the neat columns of numbers make little sense to me. Finishing up, Michael sits down across from me and waits.

I stack the ledgers. "Based on my accounting expertise, one course fifteen years ago, I'd say you don't need a banker. You need a counterfeiter."

"We've got one," he says. "I've got a twenty around here somewhere, you want to see it?" He starts to get up.

I shake my head.

"Does beautiful work," Michael says. He starts to say something else, but from outside there's a loud rumbling and shuddering, then the thump of a clutch pedal. Another truck, an old one, has pulled up next to Michael's.

He goes to the door to talk with two old men in red plaid shirts. The tall old redneck does most of the talking; the other one, fat, red-faced, looks around into the house in an offhand sort of way. When he notices me watching, he stops.

Michael leaves them at the door and gets a black leather case out of a closet. "Lyle's dog's sick," he says. The two old men drive away with us following in Michael's truck, the black case on the floorboard beside my feet. The sun is just setting and the sky is a deep red. "Dust," Michael says. "There's a front coming in."

Before long we're out of the pine forest, and the highway goes flat. In the fields on both sides there are huge dead trees and solitary, scrawny cattle. They look dead on their feet. Finally I see one move, it starts running, stops, turns, bucking and kicking. Then it stops dead again.

We park behind the old men at a house a hundred yards off the highway. The house is brick, looks almost new. The yard is just dirt, fenced with chicken wire, and a half-dozen yapping hound dogs dance along the fence. The four of us stop on the porch.

"Couldn't get Doc Milby," the tall, old redneck, Lyle, says. "Celia says he's over to Caldwell till Friday."

Michael nods. "Let's have a look."

Lyle leads us through the house, past a living room where a sixty-year-old woman sits on an old couch watching a girl watch television. The girl, in shorts, is lying on the carpet with her back against the couch and her legs across a video recorder. Michael raises a hand in the woman's direction but she doesn't blink.

Michael follows Lyle, I follow Michael, and, five feet behind me, hanging back, the other old man. He apparently assumes I'm Michael's new boyfriend.

An old hound dog lies in one corner of the kitchen on a pile of plaid flannel shirts, exactly like the shirts the two men are wearing. There's nothing obviously wrong with the dog. He just looks like he's had a real bad day. Lyle slips onto his knee and takes the dog's foreleg in one hand, showing it to Michael.

"He's a goner, sure enough," the other old man says. "Think we orta go ahead on. Shoot him."

Michael starts working on the dog's leg, rubbing up and down with both hands, pinching around the spot Lyle showed him. The dog lifts his head and Michael pets him, first his head, then grinding his fingers in the dog's fur at the shoulder. "How long ago?" he says.

" 'Bout three, four days," Lyle says.

Michael goes into his black bag for a thermometer, takes the dog's temperature. "Gonna have to pick this scab," he says. "He's abcessing."

"Damn hound's no damn good, anyway," the other man says. "Kids spoilt him. No use to anybody now. Damn sissydog."

Sneering, Lyle looks up. "J.T.," he says, "run on back to the low house, see if you can find some manners. Go on now. Don't come back till you do."

After he gets the wound to drain, Michael gives the dog a shot, then cleans up at the sink. J.T. stays in the house while we settle with Lyle on the front porch. Michael tells him to salt the dog's food for a day or so. The moon is just above the horizon, huge and bright red.

Putting away his wallet, Lyle thanks us, then takes the greasy hair behind his ear in his fingers and starts curling it elaborately, with a big slow-motion grin.

"Bows," Michael says, "you figure? Little pink bows?" He pulls his own hair, mirroring the old man. "I was fixin' to get it cut, you know? Gonna get old J.T. there to cut it, give me a permanent maybe."

"It'd be permanent all right," Lyle says.

The dogs in the dirt yard raise hell as we leave, but soon we're on the dark highway.

"*Fixin'?* You were 'fixin' ' to get your hair cut?"

Michael smiles, whipping the truck down the winding, empty country road.

In the morning Michael knocks on my door. "Let's get to it. Got breakfast cooking."

When I make it to the kitchen there are two plates on the table, each with two pieces of toast with poached eggs on top. Four eggs each plate.

"Let's hurry it up," Michael says. "Very déclassé to keep your banker waiting." He looks at me, looks at the plate. "Too much, huh?"

The drive into Austin is pleasant. Nearer the city the scenery is replaced with junkyards and an Air Force base with F-16s all lined up like toys, and the traffic gets heavier.

"Not like Houston here," Michael says. "Hondas. In Houston it's all Cutlasses. Mark's got a Mercedes, of course. Used to be you could always tell the correct car to drive by looking in Mark's garage. Jag, VW, BMW, Celica. This was his truck during the country fad."

The bank is a black glass tower. Inside there are Barcelona chairs. Michael punches the button for the elevator half a dozen times. His brother's office is on one of the lower floors.

Mark is big, not as big as Michael but maybe six one, a handsome man except for his glasses, which look like Elton John's. Mark was a year ahead of us in school, and even though he and I were both in Business, we never became great friends. He is continually fooling with the glasses, taking them off, setting them places, putting them back on.

A pretty young woman in a gauze blouse knocks and asks Mark something and he steps outside, leaving the door ajar, and says, "Tell them a hundred K and out. Bait and switch." He comes back into the office, closes the door.

"You still hustling phosphates?" he says to me.

I nod. "Just sell it, I don't formulate it. We've got a sub to do that."

"Any chance of getting on with P and G?" The glasses come off, he rubs his eyes, puts the glasses back. "Maybe they'll buy you?"

"Why buy when they can market us to death?" I am sitting while the two brothers stand, milling around the room. Michael is looking at his own work, a helicopter, hanging on one wall. Mark is looking out across an alley at a parking garage which looks like a layer cake. On another wall there's a big poster, a photograph of him in top hat and tails.

The phone buzzes and Mark picks it up, says, "Sweet surrender?" then laughs and says, "Hold them, Angelique, except the widow." He listens, laughs again, and says, "I'm putting your check in at 'Hot, All Cotton.' Putting your maillot in there too. Shrinkage what I have in mind for you, all around." He hangs up, then comes and sits on the edge of the desk near me, looks at Michael. "You think we ought to renegotiate the kid's loan? Good business?"

"Sure," I say.

"So do I," he says. "What kind of world would it be without widgets? Wooden widgets? It's just getting our vice-presidents to see our point of view. This is the third time."

"Second," Michael says. He's dusting the helicopter with his sleeve.

"Listen," Mark says, "let me send you around to talk to this friend of mine. Runs an ad agency, and between us, in desperate need of your talent. I'll call him, see if I can get you in today." He goes back behind the desk.

"Let me think about it," Michael says. "I take it that means no loan."

"No, it doesn't. It means I think it's time you got serious. Wandered into the economy. You want to be doing this ten years from now? It's clear, isn't it? It was a nice idea, but it didn't work. Time for a new idea." He shrugs. "Look, you'd turn it around, in a year you'd *be* the agency. You could write your own ticket."

"I'll think about it."

Michael picks up his ledgers. Mark looks around for his glasses, which are in his shirt pocket. "I've got a nine percent house I'll let you have," he says, "close in, three bedrooms, you can set up your saws and carve after hours."

"Technically," Michael says, starting for the door, "I don't carve. I cut."

Mark slams a drawer in the desk. "Jesus. I'll call you."

There's an elevated walkway across to the parking. The garage has low ceilings and gaudy stripes ending in arrows painted on the walls.

"He puts on that act every time," Michael says. "I can never tell whether I'm supposed to think he's the world's sexiest banker, or not a banker at all." He starts the truck and shifts into reverse. "Know one thing, though. Nothing ever gets decided in a meeting."

We stop at a downtown storefront with "ThingsInc." on the window. Michael looks at me. "Yeah, isn't that a stupid name? I'll be just a minute." He takes a package out of the back and goes inside while I wait in the truck. In twenty minutes he comes out, smiling.

"One more stop to make," Michael says, turning the truck back into the traffic. "Gotta explain to Susanna and Pedro why the checks stopped coming. And make a delivery." He waves toward the back, another package in the truckbed.

We get onto a freeway that rises up out of an older residential neighborhood as if from nowhere and drive eight or ten miles out to arrive in developer suburbs. Susanna, who I remember as a plain, red-haired girl who always looked like she hadn't had enough to eat, is on the lawn, talking to an old Chicano and one of his sons. Three more kids sit in the back of the old man's truck, along with lawn mowers, rakes, and shovels. The old man smiles as we pass him, leaving.

Susanna takes us inside where Michael's son, Peter, rushes up and jumps on Michael. The boy takes his brown-paper package and un-wraps a redwood rifle about three feet long and detailed down to a flip-up peep sight. Michael solemnly instructs Peter, who is about eight, until the child says, "Lemme have it." He takes his new toy and goes into the backyard through sliding glass doors.

Michael looks up, notices Susanna's expression. "His holiness is not going to like it?" he says.

"Earl just doesn't like guns," she says. "I agree with him. He won't say anything."

"Jesus, Susanna," Michael says. "A toy's not going to hurt him."

"We disagree," she says.

Michael gets up and goes to the glass doors. "I forgot to give him the hand grenades," he says, passing on to the terrace.

Susanna is still thin, but age has made her lovely, with bright eyes, a wry smile and her plainness, which now looks like serenity. "You're too much a stranger," she tells me. "I haven't seen you in ten years."

"More like six."

"How long are you here for?" She has gone to the kitchen, staring into a big refrigerator, brand new.

"A couple days," I say.

She lays a package of hot dogs on the formica counter in front of me, takes the last five or six out, and puts them on foil in the broiler. The soggy plastic package is a brand I don't recognize, and the date on it says, "Sell by Jan 10." It's March.

"So," she says, "how's he doing really? I mean, how bad is it?" She's holding a loaf of bread in one hand and a jar of mustard in the other. "You want chili?"

"No thanks."

"It's that Arthur person isn't it? Spending him crazy." She puts the bread and mustard down, knocking the hot-dog package off with the back of one hand. It falls into a white garbage can she's opened with her foot. "I was out there once, after the divorce, and all these trees were lying around in front of the house, you know, big brown root bags. Arthur the landscape architect. Michael told me when Arthur got it all planted it looked like L.A." She laughs. "It all died, of course. He planted them without taking the bags off or something. Then there was Arthur the jewelry designer, Arthur the printer, Arthur the submarine commander. So, you didn't answer."

"Arthur's gone," I say.

"Finally just fluttered away, I suppose." She takes a fork from the counter. "A good thing, I'd say. It was just too much, having Arthur depending on him, too."

"Too?"

"And the rest of us," she says. "I depend on him. Don't you? He's Rudolph the Red-nosed Reindeer. Temporarily short of funds. The Wizard of Oz." She's crouched down to the broiler, rolling the hot dogs around on the foil, yellow flames around her fork. "Maestro likes them burned," she says. "And, like father, like son."

"He'll be all right when he gets this loan from Mark. If he gets this loan from Mark."

"The same loan? Michael's the only one I know who can actually spend the same money three and four times. The rest of us just think about doing it."

"There's apparently some question," I say.

She shakes her head. The red hair is softer and fuller than I remember it.

She's looking out through the sliding glass over the brick terrace into the yard. Michael and Peter are in a crouching parade along a low brick wall, with green metal flowerpots on their heads. Michael turns, lifts a finger to his lips, catches Susanna and me watching. He points, drops onto his belly, out of sight, and Peter copies him. All we can see now is thrashing elbows as they crawl along the wall, and then dirt clods come arching up and land all over the terrace, shattering on the brick.

Susanna turns to me. "There's no question," she says.

When, two days later, Michael drives me to the airport, he is in a hurry. He likes to be early. We sit in the coffee shop and talk, looking idly around the small terminal. The waitress, small, square, sexy with red-tinged hair, likes Michael and they kid each other.

"She wants me," he says, to me. "I want her. Seems like a good place to stop, no? Just downhill from here."

He looks nervous. At a table behind us someone says, " . . . so he's better than me." I look around; it's a freckled, short-haired guy in white shirt and pants.

"You didn't ever want to ball me, did you?" Michael says. I don't say anything. "I thought you didn't," he says. "Relax. You're about to blow a blood vessel. This one." He reaches over and touches my forehead; I can't help jerking back.

". . . so fifty-five hours a week for nothing," the guy behind me says. "You couldn't understand it." He's talking to a woman.

Michael smiles. "I would never have gotten into it myself—queer shit—if I'd known what a lot of trouble it would cause me. But I was young, I thought I was Jesus."

They call my plane. I tip my coffee, finish it. I want to get away.

"That's not what I really hate, though," Michael says. "What I really hate is being a nice guy. Here comes Michael, the sweetheart. Roly-poly. I don't know why I can't stop. It's hopeless. Sorry. Even my name. I'd like to be Slash, or Vic, or something. Something normal." He gives me a strange look.

The freckled guy in the white outfit slams his chair into the table behind me. I'm hoping he's not on my flight, which they've just called a second time.

"I've gotta—"

"Pedro," Michael says. "Pedro'll be okay. She went and got him an asshole to be his father."

"You're a little bitter."

He's looking at me, staring, as if I'm a thief. "Yeah. Me and two hundred million others."

Of course, I'm imagining it. I stand up.

"I exaggerate," he says.

Get-together

"Patricia," he says, and his eyes get weird and his mouth falls open. He's seen the Ant Eraser—next to the salt and pepper shakers.

F.X. doesn't like ants, but he's also afraid of poisons, so I have to put out the arsenic. Like one of my fourth-graders, he's brave in big things and unnerved by small ones.

The arsenic is called Ant Eraser and comes in a small bottle, like vanilla. I put it out on cardboard on the kitchen floor, near where the cat eats. It must have sugar or something in it, because the ants leave the gourmet catfood F.X. always buys and gather around the liquid like a tiny black line of parked cars. Tonight, instead of putting the Ant Eraser away, I left it on the dinner table.

F.X. is afraid of poisons, ants, and me, now that he's having an affair. It's cruel to play on his guilt. But my alternatives are not much better. I admit my poor sportsmanship quickly. "I'm sorry. It was mean." This makes him think I'm crazy. Not what I wanted either.

F.X. is six two with blue eyes, and he can bench press 250 pounds.

That's a lot. We've been married three years. His real name is Francis Xavier. He called himself F.X. when we met, at a party.

"It's dumb, having initials," he said, "but I don't much want to be 'Francis' or 'Xavier' either, so . . . They called me 'F.X.' in high school and I got to like it."

It was raining, and after the party we went to the house he rented, an old house with a big screened-in porch where we sat in straw chairs in the dark and drank gin and Tab and talked and watched the rain until morning. Then he took me home. No bed.

We sat on that porch till late at night two, three times a week for several weeks before he got around to sex. When he drove me home, after the first night we slept together, he said, "Didn't think I could do it, did you?" We still talk, still at night, but he won't drink Tab. It's poisonous.

When he told me, he was very nervous. We were sitting at the kitchen table. I felt sexy, because I already knew. I was wearing a kimono, petting myself a little. Didn't do anything for him, so I took a little pleasure in watching him squirm. And feel sorry for me. When he told me, I laughed; I don't know why. Laughing made him worse.

"Let me guess," I said. "It's Kim, right?"

He didn't say anything, which meant I was right. He shrugged, and I was sorry I had guessed. Kim teaches exercise classes, and after F.X. took one, he talked about her. Then, when they started lifting weights together, he talked about her. Then he stopped talking about her much, so guessing was easy.

I met her once, in the supermarket. I can see why he's impressed. We stood near a checkout line and told each other that we'd heard so much about each other. That was about it. She didn't look guilty. It must have been before. I guess I thought, She's stupid—forgetting that that does not matter.

She's pretty. Maybe, prettier. She's very energetic and enthusiastic, and wears leotards, shorts, leg warmers. Nude, she probably looks like something out of a museum. I look better with clothes on. She has shoulder-length hair, brown, light. Mine is blond. Sometimes I think, How can he tell her apart from all the other joggers and weight lifters and aerobicisers? She's younger, but not enough to make much difference, a couple years. I'm thirty. I look at my breasts in the mirror and get mad, because she's making me do it.

In the supermarket she said, "He's a droll one," which struck me as strange, to hear this cheerleader using a word like *droll*. A word I don't even know how to pronounce, for certain. I never thought of him as *droll*.

They have this word together.

Kim has brown eyes. F.X. and I both have blue eyes. At the party four years ago, F.X. said he sometimes thought blue-eyed people were "weak." He meant himself, not me. You listen to all sorts of silly stuff, when you're looking for someone. Maybe it was later, on the porch, after he got a little drunk.

There was a third chair on the porch that night; the cat sat in it, his old cat. F.X. showed me how to get a cat to sit on a chair, by putting its front paws on the seat. Front paws only. It works, most of the time.

The trouble is, I like him.

When he told me, he sat across the table from me and said, "I like her and I like you." He was fidgeting with one of my hair clips, clicking it like one of those metal frogs they used to sell at Woolworth's. "I'm sorry," he said.

"Could you put that . . . down," I said, pointing to the clip.

"I don't know what to say," he said.

I sat and wished the telephone would ring, that somebody would call and interrupt. I wondered whether they talked about me. It was like being on the sidewalk looking for sunglasses or car keys and looking up, and suddenly, you're in the way.

I was staring around the kitchen, sort of vaguely. "What are you doing?" he said.

"Counting my half."

"Your half of—"

"Everything," I said.

"Patty," he said.

"You put yourself in this hole," I said. "No pun intended. Why didn't you just buy one of those blow-up dolls? Life-size." Then I started laughing again. Then I went to the store and stayed a long time.

He wants to bring the bitch here. It's her idea, I'm sure of that. We should all get together and talk things out. We're in bed when he says this. It's morning. Out the double windows beside the bed it looks like rain but it isn't raining. There's another hour before we have to dress and go to work. I get up and sit at the vanity next to the windows. The light is gray this morning.

"I don't think that'll help anything." The windows are closed. Still the air feels wet. My cotton nightgown bunches between my legs, but, rearranging it, I can't get comfortable. He's in his underwear, on one elbow on the bed, rubbing his forehead.

"It probably wouldn't help," he says. "It's probably a lousy idea. I'm sorry."

I've reconsidered by this time. Saying no to anything is bad policy, in this situation. "Okay. Let's do it. But not here. Pick some neutral ground."

"You're serious?"

"Yes, but not here. I'm pretty reasonable but not that reasonable. I don't want her flexing on my couch, petting my cat. Just thinking about it makes me want to—" I walk into the bathroom, turn on the shower, take the Pantene shampoo, behind the others, and put it out front. I think about dressing up a little, for work. Fourth-graders notice.

When I get back in the bedroom he says, "I'll arrange it." The cat, beside him, always sleeps on his side of the bed.

"What do you talk about?"

He looks at me.

"I mean, muscles? Perspiration?"

In the evening we go to a party we have to go to and I pick out a psychology professor and flirt with him. The party is spread through three big open rooms and the patio of a house by the lake. The plants in the house are all sick. The professor, Philip, sits close and tells me he is "kind." He talks about cocaine and rats. The rats are interesting, but he spends most of the time talking cocaine. I ask questions about the rats, but he sticks with the dope. He is thin, good-looking, has a fine-line moustache. He knows the names of all the sick plants, calls the false aralia "dizygotheca."

F.X.'s friend Todd stops by the couch where I'm sitting with Philip, and licks my ear when he whispers, "Have you reconsidered?" which makes me feel better. "Yes and no," I say, then, "Do that again," and he does. I look around for F.X. but can't find him.

After another half-hour of Philip, I can't stand him. "Do you want to sleep with me?" I say, and then I watch him for a couple seconds. "Is that why you've been telling me all this?" He still can't think of anything to say. "I lift weights," I say. "In the nude." He's getting up. "I get all sweaty all over." He's gone.

F.X. walks up right after and looks in the direction Philip disappeared.

"Get serious," he says. He's been waiting to leave. He waited for Philip to go. When I realize this, I begin to get insanely angry.

"I'm no charity case, fucker."

"What?"

"Take me home."

We find the car at the edge of the driveway and we each slam a door.

In the car on the way home, F.X. says, "The one I was afraid you'd find was Todd."

"I don't really need your help. But thanks anyway. Todd's fat and married."

"He was eyeing you all night," he says, shifting. The little car races along the winding streets and I remember how much he likes to drive, how well he handles cars. "When I wanted to find you, all I had to do was follow Todd's gaze. It was a gaze, for sure."

Todd has a potbelly, is very funny, has eyes like a lion, big and sleepy. F.X. said he was afraid, but he doesn't sound afraid. He sounds patronizing. So I give him something to be afraid of.

"All he has to do is ask."

"I'll tell him," F.X. says.

I wear slacks and a silk shirt, a muddy gray, thinking she'll show up in a Danskin. She doesn't. She's wearing slacks and a silk shirt. Hers is ice blue. She looks great, except for her shoes; they look like they came from Kinney's. The thunderstorms have come, and all of our shoes have taken a beating sloshing toward the restaurant F.X. has chosen for our meeting. White cotton tablecloths on the tables. We sit and stare out the windows at the lightning, the black sky, the sheets of water.

The calm which settled on him when I agreed to get together with

Kim has disappeared. I regret insisting that we do it as soon as possible. I just wanted to get it over with. We play with the silverware.

Kim is younger than I thought, and she speaks in a low voice, but fast. She has a good smile, and she manages not to touch him, which I appreciate.

The restaurant is empty because it's four in the afternoon on a Tuesday. Our waitress sits with three other employees on barstools along the bar in another part of the restaurant, rarely coming to our table. There's a TV somewhere in the bar and it's on.

Kim drinks a Tom Collins. She takes the small blue and white straw, starts to set it on the tablecloth, then holds it up. "We could draw straws," she says.

"Or flip a coin," I say.

She smiles. "Yeah, okay, have you got a quarter?"

"A quarter?"

"Okay, I'll send out for a silver dollar," she says.

"Wait a minute," F.X. says.

He's drinking iced tea, and once when he accidentally sets his glass on the edge of a spoon, all three of our hands start to shoot out to catch it. He gets it while Kim and I pull back quickly. She looks at me. "Ooops," she says. I look at F.X. I envy him. I feel tears coming but manage to stifle it.

We don't talk things out. We talk about the rain, the restaurant, the elementary school where I teach, and exercise. In the bar of the restaurant there's a small white plastic bucket into which water is dripping. The waitress and her friends don't notice it. They don't care. The roof leaks. So what. Finally Kim says, "Well, I've got to pick up my little boy," and I look outside at the wet streets and think, It should always rain. It should rain forever.

We watch Kim go. "Well," F.X. says, "you want to order something?" He picks up his knife.

Words rush through my mind, like *slut, bitch, droll, whore, hole, weak*— I can't seem to make them mean anything. I watch him; he's checking the knife, resting it across his index finger, to see where it balances. It's something he used to do. He used to do it. He told me how you do it. We were somewhere. He looks at me.

"Pick," I say, and then I feel my face twist up, I feel it around my eyes, and I begin to scream it. Pick.

The Friend

I was cruisin' in my Camaro late afternoon when a girl about nineteen I'd say, might've been older, walking down the street, pulled off to the right, I asked her if she wanted a ride, a nice thing, she was walking fast, sometimes the ones that are walking fast are real scared and won't even turn their heads, but some of them are just efficient and in that case, they're more ready to take a ride see cause they're in a hurry.

Well she said she didn't want a ride, no ride, thank you very much, she said I was clean-cut I had a coat on that's why she said that.

That's why she got into the car, because I looked like an advertiser or something like that, a disc jockey, they always accept rides from disc jockeys, that's what I told her too, that I was one. I said, "Yeah, I'm an announcer," she said "What?" I said "A disc jockey, y'know," she said "Oh yeah, really?" and I said, "What the fuck you think, I'd lie about it?" That must've been real strange I shouldn't't've said it that way, and so loud, cause she jumped when I did, when I said it. So I got real soft, talked soft and used long words, long words are just like all the others, my mother taught me them, before she was killed in the wreck. My mother and father they were real nice people, they taught me to wear a coat and how to walk like nice people and talk like nice people, and they knew, really knew how, because y'know they *were* nice people, they even had the money too, I don't know what happened to me. My sister, she taught me how to shave, she wanted to be my mother too but she couldn't, she was a nice person too, she hated it, but she's a nice person today just like she's always been. I mean she's clean. I'm clean too and slick, but I guess I'm not really a nice person.

It was getting late in the afternoon, about six I guess, and I asked her she was tanned how far she was going, the ones that are going a short way are no good because you can't talk to them, you just get something started and they get out and that's it, they say thanks a lot they never relax. But she was going a good ways, she was going to smile the whole time. "Over to the highway," she said and I said kind of casually " . . . yeah okay I'll drop you" it seemed y'know normal to say that it felt right when I said it like I was going across town. "That's a long walk," I said, "Somebody usually stops," she said, "You gotta pick out who to go with because some of them are real creeps," she said, I smiled at her.

My car is little y'know real close together, you hit their knee with your fist if you're casual about it when you're going for third gear. If you're clumsy they get scared but if you're casual they don't take much notice, takes care of your hands. If you wanted to you could just grab them right there but you have to drive, you need them to drive you might hit a big Oldsmobile parked, a little wreck maybe, but nothing would ever get done just the same.

The car's blue, a deep blue not dark or light really and the interior's blue too. She was real pretty in the car, she fit her butt down into the bucket seat real nice and moved every little bit, to make me feel it, she didn't do it for that reason but I liked thinking so that she did. She had sandy brown hair, long they all have long hair, and her butt in tight jeans blue tight blue, and a silky brown shirt, I don't know why a nice girl like her would be riding with someone but they all do it now, I see them along the street every day, some of them even hitchhike.

I offered her a cigarette a Marlboro they all smoke Marlboro if they smoke, some of them don't even smoke, there were some foreign ones on the dash in the blue pack just in case she'd say "I'll have one of *these*," but she wasn't like that, she took the Marlboro, and I hit the lighter. She was real nice, she waited for the lighter, I hate those pushy ones who light their own after you went to the trouble to push in the lighter. They're always surprised, happy surprised when you smoke Marlboro because that's their brand of course and it makes them feel closer to you, maybe they don't think that way but that's the way they feel down in their sweet bodies they feel it.

The radio light was blue on her legs on the jeans they were some kind of soft material, she was a soft girl, they were soft blue material that kind of shined when the radio light hit it. There were a lot of trees it was in a nice neighborhood. I live in a nice neighborhood on purpose I don't want burglars around stealing my equipment, I got a lotta nice equipment. The trees were all spaced out in the lawns, looked like they were planted that way on purpose, the grass was almost as neat as the trees. But you can tell if you look real close, that somebody planned the trees, even if you're not used to looking for it, if you just kind of glance even though it was getting darker, the sun changed colors it was gold brown it was about six o'clock I think.

God she was nice. She had on this brown silk shirt, I've always meant to get a shirt that color, one like that. I had a yellow one I was going to dye but I never got around to it. You can tell if you're beside them whether they've got any tits or not you've got sense you can't tell they'll get red there's never enough time, you can't tell whether they're smooth, you got to guess at that, but you can tell whether they've got any, she had tits not a whole lot but respectable, she was respectable I wouldn't've picked her up if she wasn't if she hadn't been. I guess she was smooth respectable girls are smooth usually, her skin looked real smooth on her soft face, where it slipped under her shirt it was smooth I wouldn't've picked her up if it wasn't.

College she was in college I went to college it wasn't a good college but they don't care about good colleges anywhere except at Harvard there they always care. I learned a lot of stuff in college about being clean, but not too clean, those too clean people scare me like they're going to go screaming crazy and slice you with an axe, a big silver axe that shines on both sides, those guys with short hair and dull cars.

I didn't finish, college I mean, I got through a year, but I still can vote like they say on the radio, if they ever catch me I won't be able to I know that, they'll lock me up with those angry people and I won't be able. I've never voted yet but if somebody I really liked was up I'd vote for him I'd even vote for a woman, women are real nice, I'd vote for one if I liked her I'd vote for her if she was soft I'd probably like to vote for her.

I learned a lot of stuff in college, but what I was trying to tell about was the rule, the rule is that there's nothing behind all that stuff they tell you to do, they can't do anything but threaten you and if you don't get edgy about what they're threatening you with then you don't have to do it or not do it depending on whether it's something you can do or can't do according to them. It's like all those people, nice people got together and agreed to do some things and not to do other things, and they never asked me about it so I don't have to do it so long as I'm not worked up over what they're threatening me with you understand. Or if they don't catch me, it's both. I stayed inside for years, I think what I was doing was cleaning all the shit out of my mind that they put into it, like that you had to do this and you couldn't do that because we'd agreed when I hadn't agreed at all I never agreed.

She had the nicest soft sandy colored hair and she had a nice voice I like girls with nice voices and she had a nice voice it wasn't real high and screechy but it was low sort of, and happy, I like happy girls. She moved kind of slowly like she was respectable because she was it was obvious to me. Every time you stop at a light you got to be careful because they might want to get out, they change their minds real quick if you get edgy but I wasn't edgy because she was going a good ways, if I hadn't stayed in the house those three years I wouldn't've forgot all the nice things I learned, or they would be more important or something, but I had so I had to have one going a long way so I could get up to talking pretty free, it takes me a while.

So I ran a lot of yellow lights, amber, I know that, the lights aren't really yellow, that's another thing just like the sun, but they teach you about the sun, they're real proud of that, y'know about not rising and setting, and they don't about the lights and oh God all sorts of other shit you got to find out for yourself it's a lot of work and not worth it especially if you didn't sign that paper, the agreement, and I'm not going to do any of it I don't feel like, if I'd signed I'd do it because I signed it, but I haven't and I don't think I would now because I'm doing better without it. Only thing is everybody else signed it seems like, so it's real hard to talk to them, you got to play like you signed some times.

It was Thursday afternoon, almost night and the streets were pretty empty of people, it was getting dark, but I could still see y'know that there weren't many cars of course everybody was home eating. They eat balanced meals, something white and something green and something red. I eat balanced meals too because I don't want to get sick, if you get sick you have to lie around and I already did enough of that staying home three years.

The funny thing was that when we'd pass a girl driving alone I'd still want to look, to see what she looked like, I've watched and other guys do that too even when they've got one of their own right with them. It's probably pretty insulting to do that so I cover up the looking by making it part of something else like checking for traffic.

The trouble with having to have all that time to get talking, beside that you need one going a long ways, is that you got to keep good control all the time, your hands mostly, that's the first thing, it's the same way trapping anything, I guess that's why the Indians were so good they could wait and wait and wait.

The streets change over toward the highway, they get wider and dirtier but not too dirty, but not clean like in the nice section where I picked her up in her brown shirt and tight jeans and soft sweet skin at the neck. I didn't want to let her off on the dirty streets because the clean people should stay in the clean section and the dirty people in the dirty sections, the dirty people stay pretty much in their section and kill each other, when they kill a clean one they write it up real big in the newspapers for weeks and weeks, but the clean people they think they own everything and they expect they can go to any section and do anything they want to there like I remember I used to think that too the way I used to be I used to drive around. And one time not too long ago I was riding down a highway I used to hitchhike and I didn't feel that I owned it any more, I used to own all this I thought but I didn't feel it because really I don't. But some of the clean people, people with money, expect they own it all their life, people who know the governor or something, those people ought to be killed, because that's not true.

Anyway I was going to have to let her off if I couldn't get onto the highway first, if the light was red, or I'd have to run the light and there might be a cop so I slowed down, gradually I slowed down because it was real red. So I slowed way down because I could see it was far off red, she was beginning to get the idea I think because she was moving around in the bucket seat so sweet tight blue jeans made out of some kind of soft material hard to get down unless we could get it decided beforehand.

Well the light turned all right, and it didn't matter I didn't have to speed up because it was a long light, at the highway, we were talking about records because I told her I was a disc jockey. I had to tell her I liked all that drooly shit because I knew she liked it, I wished she didn't but they always do, and it makes them feel closer to you when you like it too, but I hate to tell them I like that shit I like more angry shit, mean, but I tell them something maybe one thing which is something I really think at the same time so that makes it almost all right so I made the turn, so I headed up the ramp onto the highway.

When they get the idea and you're on the clean highway and there's only space on either side and it's dark and you're inside the dark car just me in the light coat and slacks and her in the soft jeans and silk shirt in that little half-lighted space, they pretty quickly figure they're not going to get out of it, and she did she was real good because she realized real quick without talking about it, what was happening to her, I hate the ones that act outraged and scream at you "What're you doing!" like they don't know exactly what you're doing what you're going to do. I hate those. So she starts talking to you about it, soft, like "You don't really want to . . . " and like that, or like "Why do you do this?" like she really wants to know why, if she's going to get raped she wants to know why I'm going to rape her although it's probably the first time she's ever been raped, that's what everybody calls it, I call it that I don't care.

I tell her I'm not really a disc jockey, I admit it, but she likes it, she looks glad that I told her, not glad really but better than she looked before I told her. And because I already smoke her brand of cigarettes and because we like the same music and because she knows I'm pretty set on getting it from her and because we're out in the middle of nowhere and because after I pull off onto a back road and off the back road I get around the little car quicker than she can get out and run because she doesn't have it quite planned out, she takes it almost easy and I try to be as nice as I can and not hurt her too bad and I feel real good coming inside her way down inside coming inside her, rising on my hands afterward rolling over off her afterward. Her brown shirt pushed up over her soft tits, it's like a lot of times when I was in high school out on the deserted street in my car I was scared then but now I'm not scared much it only takes ten minutes or so.

Some of them scream the whole time and kick, and that's all right I mean it's like in the movies when the guy says *I love it when they scream* . . . it's true, you do, or maybe that's not in the movies maybe I just made that up myself I don't know, but it's better when they move a lot, they get moving up and back with their sweet bodies, and crying and a little sweat on their lip their forehead, they have needs too, maybe they're even being nice to you because you need so much it feels the same either way. Their shirts their skirts pushed up over their chests all that soft body for your hands God it feels good.

When we get back into the car she's quiet, crying a little but that's all, and I'm quiet too I just want to *drive* but I can't drive too fast because of cops they would ruin it. And so I take her back to where she wanted to be, because I like her and I let her off and I stop her and say just to her and quiet and quick "I'd liked to know you and do it that way but that way only lasts three weeks it's only good for three weeks or so that's all," because that's what I believe.

Chat

When Wilkens took it to the university, the cat refused to talk. The secretary sneezed for the full twenty minutes Wilkens and the cat waited in the outer office. The professor, a primatologist, pulled at his tie, yellow with red orangs, and said, "Yes, an exceptional animal. Perhaps he's just tired. Or something. They get tired, you know." As Wilkens was leaving, he heard the professor say to his secretary, "Like I said—a flake."

The cat had wandered into Wilkens' garage and rubbed up against the screen door. Others had done the same thing through the years, but this one was black with blue eyes. He had never seen a blue-eyed black cat before. He had let the cat in and taken it to the veterinarian for shots. Even the veterinarian had thought the cat's eyes unusual. That was three years ago.

The first thing Wilkens had heard the cat say was, "What you think is that I *like* eating off the floor?"

He was sitting at the kitchen table at the time. He had just fed the cat, and the cat was looking at the pink mush in its bowl. Wilkens was coaxing it. "What's the matter with that?" he had said. Then the cat said what it said.

"What?"

"Ooops," the cat said.

The cat refused to say anything more. Wilkens had a bourbon to steady his nerves and tried to get the cat to speak further, but it was adamant. It meowed. It ate dinner. It wandered off into the back of the house, fell asleep on the CD player. He went to bed, locking the cat out of the bedroom.

For several weeks he tried to get the cat to say something else. He tried to place the cat's accent, which had sounded vaguely British, albeit in miniature. Finally, he threatened to give the cat away.

"I'm taking you to the Humane Society."

The cat ignored him, dragged itself across the oriental rug with its front paws, sharpening its claws. "That's genuine!" Wilkens cried. He took the cat to the Humane Society.

The woman at the Humane Society wore a tattoo on each bicep. She smiled and said, "Are you sure this is a stray?" The woman had to drag the cat away. When she released it and picked up her pen, the cat ran back across the counter. It trembled and tore Wilkens' shirt sleeve as she pulled on its hind legs. "He seems very attached to you," the woman said.

"I checked Stray, there," Wilkens said, pointing to the box on the form he had filled out.

"When you adopt an animal, it's just like marriage," the woman said. "For richer or poorer."

Two other women with tattoos had gathered behind the counter, petting the cat. It shied away. It looked terrified.

"This is a legal document," the first woman said. "That's love, in his eyes." The cat's blue eyes were watering. Two additional women had come in the main entrance and now stood on either side of it.

Wilkens took out a cigarette. Without looking, the woman pointed to a NO SMOKING sign on the wall behind her.

She stared at him. "This information is accurate?"

Because he had momentarily forgotten whether nodding the head or shaking the head was the affirmative gesture, Wilkens only grunted.

"You gave Jake away?!" Wilkens' sister said. "You know what they do down there? They put them in a big jar and suck all the air out. They suffocate him."

"There were extenuating circumstances," he said.

"What?" his sister said. "Like what?" His sister a powerfully attractive woman with a penchant for "Stallone films," as she liked to call them. A woman of action.

"How can I get him back?" Wilkens said.

"Me," his sister said. "Just hope they haven't . . . Leave it to me."

His sister brought the cat home, took his check. After his sister left, the cat said, "We must work something out." Wilkens recognized the accent. The cat must have gotten it from the television. Sheik Yamani.

There were things the cat wanted to know.

"Why does your sister have such an elegant car when you have only this shably one?"

"That's 'shabby.' The word is 'shabby.' "

"Shabby, then," the cat said. "Why is it?"

"She has a better job than I do. She earns more money."

"Ah," the cat said.

There were things Wilkens wanted to know.

"You *can* talk," he said.

"Any six-month-old kitten can talk," the cat said.

"Why, then, don't they?"

"It just isn't done," the cat said. "You could get me one of those?"

"This is bourbon," Wilkens said.

"Some cream in it, please."

Wilkens poured the bourbon at the counter, stepped toward the refrigerator, then stopped.

"Milk will do, in lieu of cream," the cat said.

"Your species is giving our species the silent treatment, then," Wilkens said, when he sat back down at the table.

"I would not put it that way," the cat said. "You set a great store by talking, don't you? What's a species?"

"Why wouldn't you talk when I took you to the university? To that snotty monkeyman? You made me look like an idiot."

"You are an idiot, aren't you?" the cat said.

"And you never talk in front of my sister."

"Your sister is surely an idiot."

"Hey," he said, raising his fist.

The cat drew back, baring its teeth, the black fur bristling along its spine. "Try it," the cat said. Wilkens dropped his fist. "I have ants in the brain," the cat said.

Wilkens stared.

"Ants in my brain."

"I don't understand," Wilkens said.

"I am unhappy. No one really loves me."

"I love you."

"You took me to be gassed," the cat said. "You don't let me go outside."

"The traffic," Wilkens said. "You'd get run over."

"A lot you would care," the cat said. "There are ants in my food."

"Is that like ants in the brain?"

The cat sighed, looked at the ceiling. "No, that's like little black things crawling over the tuna fish."

Wilkens watched the cat blink; the left eye seemed to trail behind, a microsecond slower than the right. With its eyes fully open again, the animal appeared to have developed a grin, which to Wilkens looked patronizing. "You eat at the table now, though."

"And I appreciate it."

Wilkens smiled.

"You turn the air conditioner off when you leave the house. It's August, you know."

"Okay, I'm sorry," Wilkens said. "It was the money. The bill. But . . . I'll leave it on from now on."

"I'm sorry to complain so much," the cat said. "I know it makes me even less attractive than I am."

"You're beautiful; you're the handsomest . . . cat . . . I've ever seen."

"You say that, and I try to believe it, but why does everyone treat me like a leper?"

"Those women at the Humane Society loved you."

"No, they didn't. They just hated you. They were bitches, anyway."

"At least we agree on something," Wilkens said.

"I attract bitches. Like your sister. I mean," the cat said, "she's nice, but Christ, kittykitty this, kittykitty that, what a moron. You are not a cat. There's no way you could know what it's like down here."

"Bad, huh?"

"And where does she get those weird clothes?"

"Army-Navy," Wilkens said. "Many people affect—"

"There're copies of *Gung Ho* under the seat of her car. I looked. This job she has, she is some kind of spy or something?"

"Actually," Wilkens said, "she works for a bank."

"Even you," the cat said, "you would not care for me if I did not have blue eyes, isn't that right?"

"I had no idea you suffered so."

The cat stopped, stared at him. "Why do you think I sleep all the time?" The cat's blue eyes shone.

"I hadn't thought—"

"You like me only because I am not ordinary," the cat said. "You whore after unusual or odd things. As does your sister, who dresses in camouflage gear and reads mercenary magazines. You spend your time somewhat desperately trying to find things most other people do not like, or own . . . yet. You spent a thousand dollars on that hideous little rug simply and solely because it came from the Far East. Your shoes are Belgian. When everyone else had burnished silver stereo components, you bought black. Given an idea from a Dakota and an idea from Deauville, you'd take the French one for no other reason than that it was imported, so to speak. This is pathetic, no? This hurts you. It's a sort of bondage. Speaking of which, the other morning, quite by accident I wandered into your closet, and —" The cat finally looked up into Wilkens' fierce eyes, and immediately arched its back and threw its shoulder so high so quickly it could feel ligaments tearing. "Forget it," the cat said. "Never mind. I didn't mean anything by—"

"Shut up," Wilkens said.

"As you wish," the cat said. "I was simply making my point. What I have been doing is what you customarily use your precious 'talk' for, is it not? Whining, disguised as self-analysis. Humiliation, disguised as helpful hints. Leaving aside obscurantism, mendacity, rodomontade." The cat stretched, luxuriously.

"Sometimes," Wilkens said, "we make jokes."

The cat yawned. "Wake me for the jokes," it said.

Samaritan

America was full of fat people taking baths. I was watching them with binoculars from a large seventh-floor office in a new professional building in a good section.

My patient Mr. R comes each Monday, Wednesday, and Friday and spends the day in the chair. He does not like to lie down. Mr. R thinks I am a psychiatrist. He is wrong, of course; Mr. R is wrong about everything.

Mr. R is a heavyset male, about six feet, with slightly wavy slightly long blond hair, who wears shades when the sun is very bright.

"She said my eyes looked bad. She said the evil showed in my eyes—"

"Nancy?" I said. Nancy is Mr. R's wife. Nancy R.

"No," he said. "My mother. My mother told me that when I was eighteen."

"What was the evil she was talking about?"

"I was screwing some sweet little thing. It was obvious somehow."

"You're twenty-seven years old."

"God, I know. Do you think I can get back into law school?"

"I don't think it would be healthy. Why do you remember at this time something your mother said to you almost ten years ago?"

"I don't know," he said. "I mean, I'm not sure." Mr. R is leaning a little forward in the armchair. He is thinking. "Are you directive?"

"No."

"I think I said it because I talked to her last week. On the telephone. She's in Santa Barbara." Mr. R cannot help indicating the direction of Santa Barbara by gesture. "She asked me if she had done it to me, fucked up my life. She said she had done her best, the best she knew. She wanted me to tell her if it was her fault."

"If what was her fault?"

"Me—me—if I . . . if my problems were her fault. What could I say?"

"No."

"That's what I said. Sort of."

I glanced at the clock on my desk; it was late. White numerals. "It's near twelve," I said. "Let's break for lunch. Be back here at one-thirty."

Mr. R was very thankful, for the morning. That's normal. Mr. R is usually thankful for the morning. In the afternoon he is often angry, I think because he glimpses that his problems are very involved and complex and may well take a very long time to resolve in an acceptable way. In the morning he is usually thankful because he knows that if he is not I will punish him during the afternoon.

During lunch Mr. R drives home and takes a bath, eats whatever Nancy (Nancy!) has prepared for him, reads, returns, and waits in the outer office. I am there the whole time, with the binoculars, eating fitfully at the sliced barbecue which I have paid for with Mr. R's money, and taking a Valium, 20 mg. If when he returns R parks in the west lot, I can pick him up as he turns off Thirty-fourth, the perfect swing of the Lincoln into a parking space, the expression on his face as he gets out, the strong stride toward the building. He looks healthy. I can imagine what it's like talking to crazy people all day long. I much prefer the sane sober ones like Mr. R, and the state wants you to have a license. Mr. R has bought up all my Mondays,

Wednesdays, and Fridays for over a year and there is no sense taking the risks involved in seeing other patients. I am not greedy. I congratulate myself on my sensible attitude.

At two o'clock Miss Davies (Brenda!) tells me that he is back. He has been back for half an hour. Sweet Brenda and I are finishing up. Trading off on the binoculars. Interplay. Balling seven stories in the air, looking at each other and at the wildly potent city through the huge bluish sheets of plate glass. "Think of me as a doctor." And she does. She makes phone calls while we're making it, in the old style. She pretends disinterest. Pauses. Sweet Brenda is a lover, and a lover of irony with a degree in psychology. Silver buttons all down her back.

I can appreciate it. How fresh Mr. R looks when he returns for the afternoon. A clean shirt (R has a great many). A shave. The Valium is spinning around in my brain and I can appreciate practically anything. At three-thirty, Stelazine. At five, a Triavil 4-10 so I don't fall asleep on the way home. I bathe, and at six-thirty show up at Lisa's for dinner. All my early life I spent working toward a lady named Lisa. And, for the most part, she has made good, although in a somewhat different way than expected. All that time in Mass General, where when we got the brain in view, I could never figure out what was what. And God, it was nauseating. You can't imagine how disgusting the naked brain. But I never vomited. I mean you get in there, and you can't tell which is which and what the grease does. ("Doctor, what's that yellowish stuff . . . No, no, the grease over he—" He hit my hand.) I didn't last.

At Lisa's there is booze, a drink and then dinner. She can cook. She is civilized, sweet and civilized. She has a second-story place, two paneled rooms with a kitchen and a flat roof where you can fuck in the wind. There is also a lake, water through the trees. Whoever is up can watch the water if she or he wants. On the roof, super natural. Lying back looking at the sky, and it's cold in the fall. In the winter you freeze, so we stay inside. Sometimes it rains. Lisa loves me. I worked long and hard to get where I am.

Mr. R looks fresh and clean at two when I step to the door of the waiting room and nod slightly toward him, wait, then turn and follow him down the hallway and into my office, like his father. I seat myself behind the desk while he is still standing. Mr. R has a fetish about this; he must always be the last to sit down. He is a large man, several years younger than I, but filled out as in maturity in a politician. In fact, I think he is a lawyer, has a firm, real estate, oil, other interests. Friendly with the great and powerful. Once I was afraid of Mr. R, but I have come a long way, and I have shown him—rather, pointed at him—the Smith and Wesson, and the dominance situation has been clearly understood ever since.

Finally he sits down, relaxes back into the big chair which situates him most nearly opposite the door, lays his filterless Chesterfields and matches on the glass table. He tightens a little and leans forward in the chair. Rearranges the cigarettes a little farther away from the pot which holds the plastic plant. The walls are wood. We are subdued.

"You were speaking about your eyes . . ."

He remembered the morning's session. "Oh my God, can we talk about something else?"

"Surely," I said. "But there seems to be some energy here and we might be able to make use of it."

"Okay," he said. "Okay." He takes a Chesterfield out, effortlessly, without moving the pack. For a moment, I hate his guts. But the feeling never makes it to my face and I cover easily by beginning to speak.

"Your eyes?"

"Oh yeah." He takes a long first drag on the cigarette and drops his hand. "Well, it wasn't much, it was just something my mother said to me when I was graduating from high school—"

"Do you know why you are reluctant to talk about it?"

"I'm not. I mean not really. I'm reluctant to talk about my mother, really."

"Were you close to your mother?"

"Yeah, I guess, close enough. Up until high school. You know, I started getting laid. I started exaggerating, you know, lying. I started sucking up to the other kids instead."

"Instead of . . . "

"Instead of to them."

"I would say that what you describe is a fairly common process. Your family was well-to-do?"

"Yeah, well enough. My old man runs a mud company."

Mr. R has made a joke. "A mud company?"

"Yeah, yeah, he sells mud. They shove it down oil wells. Keeps the drill bits cool."

"Did you get along with him?"

He hesitates. "Yeah, we got along pretty well. We used to go hunting. We had a dog, a shepherd named King, and I wanted to take him hunting but Dad said we couldn't. He had a lot of reasons, good reasons, he was right."

Mr. R stops and gets himself another cigarette, slowly. He looks as if he can't decide whether or not to light it. "He got hit by a car. King. One Sunday he got hit. I found him up against the gate, whimpering, there was a lot of blood on the walk. We rushed him to the vet, carried him in and laid him on this stainless steel table. He was every once in a while raising his head, swinging it up a little and kind of whimpering to me, but mostly he just lay there. The vet stuck a needle in him. King just lay there on the table, and then he shook a little, shuddered, and all this blood and crap started coming out, blood out of his mouth and crap falling out of his ass and he was still in it, and didn't move. I helped the vet put him into a big black plastic bag and he tied it up and we carried it out to the back and put it inside a freezer with some others. Then we left. My old man had to drive the car, but I just sat there in the front seat and didn't have anything to do. And, you know what was funny about it?" he said. "What was funny about the whole thing?"

"What?"

"—That week . . . my only reaction to all that, was one night I broke up, crying and sobbing and choking and all that shit, and the only thing that came to my mind was 'He was just a dog. He was just a goddamned dog . . . ' " Mr. R is looking at me asking some question.

"Because he was not responsible . . . didn't deserve . . . "

"Yeah, yeah! Like he wasn't responsible for anything because he was just a goddamn dog, he didn't do anything that justified getting mauled that way. So I went out and started digging up the street with a pick. I was digging a rut across it in front of the house so you'd have to drive real slow. But my old lady saw me and said a lot of stuff about how I'd cause a wreck and somebody might get killed and the street wasn't ours, so I stopped. She was right. I started hating the dog."

He was making me nervous, moving around too much, making

gestures which were unusually harsh. "Let's quit for the afternoon," I said. "I don't think we can get anything more done this afternoon."

"Okay," he said. "Okay." Relaxing back into the chair. "That's crazy, isn't it?"

"I think your behavior was normal, under the circumstances. I don't see anything else you could have done. Everyone uses unusual methods when put into strong stress situations."

"No, no, I mean about the dog. I mean *hating the dog* . . . "

"That is what I was talking about," I said. "Let's quit for today."

After he left I got another Valium and asked Brenda to transcribe the tapes before she went home. At street level I went into a telephone booth and called Lisa at work.

"Hey, lady, you've got the afternoon off."

"I can't . . . "

"Oh yeah you can; you've got to see a doctor. He's liable to die if you don't. Pick you up in twenty minutes . . . "

Then I dialed Nancy.

"Chico, is that you?"

"Yeah, just thought I'd call. He's coming at you."

"Why, what for? You get tired of hearing him whine?"

"Sweet young thing, aren't you?"

"Speaking of which, how's that tanned little number in your office?"

"Look, Nancy, he's coming home, just thought I'd alert you. Broaden your awareness a little."

"What happened? Why so early?"

"A . . . well, he started telling me about this dog he had when he was a kid . . . Oh God. He ever tell you about that?"

"About 'King.' About 'King' getting run over?"

"Yeah. He started—What are you laughing at? What's so fucking funny?"

"Did he get any? Get into your pants?"

"I think I've got the wrong number."

"Listen honey, he made himself king of the Phi Delts with that story."

"Yeah, well, what were you going to be when you grew up? Hey look, I'm not gonna make it tomorrow. I've got too much to do. Next week, okay?"

"Finally," she said.

"Finally what?"

"Finally we get to the purpose of this call."

"Only to hear the soothing sweetness of your voice."

I left, picked up Lisa at her office and drove to her house in the suburbs. On Thursday I called the office and asked Brenda to call R and tell him that his Friday appointment was postponed. On Saturday Lisa went to the grocery store. On Sunday we turned the lights back on.

"God, it's bright in here."

"Where's the *TV Guide?*" she said, in a long brown gown. She turned off some lights. "I threw it on the floor . . . here it is." She picked it up. White sun-colored hair, nothing so sweet in this whole world as a rich girl.

"Hey, lady, come lie down so's I can disrobe you . . . Is that right? Can I 'disrobe' you? Sounds disgusting."

"How about Tony Franciosa and Dean Martin?"

"Wonderful. C'mon and lie down. What's it called?"

"*Career.* Chico, I've been lying down for *four days.*"

"Wanna go for the record?"

"God, Chico, where'd you get to be so *quick.* Quicker than a speeding—"

"Yeah, well, I used to be quick. But you know, an agile mind's . . . "

"What is the matter with you?" She looked at me.

"I had a bad week. But if you'll lie your slinky body down right here . . . "

"That's lay."

I looked at her.

"Don't say it," she said.

Monday morning, Mr. R came in and worried about his daughter, seven. Brenda worried about her boyfriend. I took a few of these and a few of those and didn't worry. I was all right. Happy, perhaps.

By eleven-thirty, I felt that the whole daughter thing was getting silly, and so I provided a solution, a temporary one. Most solutions are.

"Look, how old is she?"

"Seven," he said.

"All right, then, you've got five or six years before it really becomes a problem, right? Right now her problems are on about the *doll* scale. I can't see any advantage in rushing it. Perhaps she'll be ugly." An insensitive remark.

"Look," he said.

"Mr. R," I said. "If you're not willing to deal in the general area . . . I would be curious to know what connection there is between your child's future sexual adjustment, a problem that is in large measure several years off, and the matters we have been discussing these last few months."

"Yeah, yeah. I'm sorry. I've got a lot of things on my mind. I wasn't thinking." He was smoking and standing up. He was leaving.

"I realize that it is important, but it seems that, for our purposes, the time could be better spent, and that we might be discussing this to avoid discussing something else. Anyway, why don't we try again this afternoon?" This jargo-spanking made us both unhappy. I felt incautious. He was taking everything much too seriously.

At lunch Brenda attacked with questions about Mr. R. She is taking her second degree, and doing very well. She has a healthy natural curiosity. A rare thing in a healthy girl. I do my best. Slate black hair and deep green eyes.

"How would you characterize his case?" she said.

"His case. Yes, well, I would say that R's problem has something to do with the fact that he's just like everybody else. Success is his problem. No, that's wrong. R's problem is that he is just like everybody else and *he doesn't like it*."

"He can't adjust?" she said.

"Adjustment," I said. "Adjustment is precisely the problem. It doesn't work."

"For very long. It's not permanent."

"Exactly, beautiful. *You* have hit on it. And somehow Mr. R was convinced by something or someone that adjustment was, in fact, permanent. And past that, that it worked. A cruel joke on him, but a bit of good luck for you and me."

"Isn't it a little dishonest?" she said.

"Yes. A little. But you know, so is bowling. One does better not to worry too heavily about his honesty. One tends to discover that all his crimes are petty ones. Okay?"

"I know what you mean," she said.

"That makes one of us," I said. "Could I have one last taste of that there?"

At one-thirty R came back, sweating. At two, he came into my office and sat down. Then stood up. We talked for about half an hour. He walked around the office, smoking, picking things up to look at them. He talked. And finally he sat down, as if very tired, and was silent for a long time, perhaps ten minutes.

"Doctor. You were asking, last week, about what I wanted to do with analysis . . ."

"I don't think I quite understand."

He settles on the forward part of the big armchair. "I mean you asked me what I wanted ultimately to achieve, through being here, through seeing you." Massive, blond.

"Yes."

"Well, I don't think I'm going to make it. I don't think I'm going to be able to do it." He tightened a fist and stared down at it. Quiet.

Then he began again. "I saw this movie on television. Did you ever see that Zapata movie? With Marlon Brando?" He was leaning forward; I slid the desk drawer open.

I nodded. "I've seen it . . ."

"*That's* who I want to be!" he says. Falls back into the chair, relaxing; he has gotten a clear statement of purpose out.

Watching this bizarre performance, easy and uneasy.

"Like in the scene," he says, "where they're bringing him in—Brando—and all the peons are there, crouched over, and they start clapping the stones together until all you can hear are the horses' hooves and the stones clapping . . .

"Or, oh God!" he says, "the best scene—the scene where the soldiers—"

"Diaz's army . . ."

"Yeah, or whoever they are, they're riding in this double column with Zapata on foot in the middle, and one of them has—"

Staring at a circular glass ashtray to the left on my desk which cost eighteen dollars.

"—this rope which is around his neck, and they're riding down this narrow road through some hills dragging him along with his hands tied behind him, and down from the hillsides come the peons in the white pants and white shirts, and they're only carrying machetes while the soldiers have rifles, but they just keep coming, walking alongside the columns of soldiers, until there're about a hundred of them, and there're only about fifteen or twenty soldiers, and the soldiers are still riding along just real slow like they have been the whole time, not even looking at the peons with their machetes . . . "

I cured him. It was easy. I just opened the drawer, took the .38 out, aimed it at his forehead, and blew a big hole in it, a little right of center.

He was so wound up, so oblivious to everything, that it was really quite simple to get the gun out of the drawer and squeeze off a loud and easy shot into his brain before he said, or thought of, whatever it was he was going to say, eventually.

That's No Reason

"Don't get hooked on me, Alex," she said, just across the Tennessee line, and he began laughing and almost ran over a Honda ahead of them in the lane.

When he calmed down enough to talk he saw the way she was looking at him and tried to explain. "I used to get in trouble for saying that exact same thing, to women. I was told it was insulting."

"I just don't feel like a relationship."

He laughed again; she looked at him again.

"It's funny. Just trust me."

Three days traveling with the girl before she asked him what he did; Alex picked her up outside a highway hamburger place in Baton Rouge on his dead brother's birthday, July thirty-first, and they got into Charlottesville on the third of August.

"Nothing," he said. "I'm independently wealthy." He looked into her eyes, to see how she took it.

She had the bluest eyes. He had seen sapphires once, in a hippie jewelry store, stood around a half-hour carefully inspecting tray after tray of stones, pretending to a hairy clerk that he was in the market when he really couldn't have afforded a piece of faceted quartz.

Her eyes were sapphire blue, and her skin was freckled and her hair was dull and brown. She could wash it, he thought; but she did wash it, in the motel showers.

They had been driving eight hours a day and spending the nights at motels, with liquor they bought along the way, having learned to get it early so as not to have to drive all over some strange town once they got where they were going.

They would settle in at a motel, outside Birmingham, Knoxville, now in Charlottesville, turn on the TV, lie back and douse the night with Scotch and sex and television, and sleep. The next morning around eleven, on the road again, stopping midway for a bottle of Glasgow or the Pride of Baltimore.

"You're a drifter," she said, and her eyes glowed.

He laughed. "They have drifters in movies. Westerns, usually."

"You think everything I say to you is funny."

"Just about," he said.

"I don't care what you are."

"I'm a driver. A motorist." He smiled.

He had had jobs; teacher, media buyer, real-estate salesman, assistant manager, bartender, bartender, bartender. He couldn't sleep. He drank too much.

The first night, when she undressed, he laughed when he saw the leopard-skin panties she was wearing, and that almost put an end to their relationship right there, but getting insulted must have seemed like too much effort — she laughed too and he said he didn't mean anything by it.

"Aren't you going to call your brother's friend?" she said, on the bedspread in Charlottesville, in new underwear she'd taken from the duffel bag that leaned against the curtains over the front windows.

"Tomorrow," he said. "He's a Republican."

The girl frowned. "What's a Republican?"

He had told her he was going to see a friend of his brother, a Marine. His brother, Billy, killed, Parrot's Beak, Cambodia, 1970.

Alex and the girl had driven up through Washington, found a liquor store on Connecticut Avenue, driven past the White House and Lincoln, stopped at the Vietnam Memorial and looked for Billy's name. There were too many people and he was hot and hungry; they left without finding it. He bought a half-pound of roast beef in a delicatessen and ate it in the air-conditioned car on the way back down to Charlottesville, dropping the cold red slices into his mouth one by one, looking up, and chasing them with Diet Coke.

"Sure you don't want some?" he said.

"It poisons the body."

"Body gets poisoned, one way or the other," he said.

"Watch the road, would you please?"

He brought the big Oldsmobile back into lane.

"What was it like? Vietnam?"

"Hey, honey, I didn't go."

"Sure were a lot of names," she said, turning her sapphire eyes on him.

In the evening they lay together on the blue velour bedspread and watched the television, a movie, *Ordinary People*, until it was too late to call a Republican.

"That's what it was like," she said, pointing to the TV. On the screen Mary Tyler Moore looked like she'd spent the day at the taxidermist. It took Alex a minute to realize the girl wasn't talking about the same "it" as earlier.

"That's what what was like?"

"My old lady," she said.

"Bullshit. Everything you say is bullshit."

She got off the bed and walked to the bathroom. "Geezer," she said, and slammed the bathroom door. Alex switched channels.

After twenty minutes, when she still had not come out, he took the bottle he'd bought in the city and knocked on the bathroom door with it. When the door opened a crack, he pushed the bottle in.

"Poison the body," he said. "Your mother's a—a creep. A slug-sucker. A waxoid."

"A what?"

"Made it up," he said.

She took the bottle and opened the door, took a drink, dribbling it on her freckled chest. She looked around the tiny bathroom.

"Poison the body," she said, raising the bottle a second time.

When Billy had gone down to enlist in the Marines he was so spooky, it was easy to think they wouldn't take him, even then, when they were taking everybody.

One minute Billy talked about freezing a ball of peanut butter and swallowing it—supposed to show up on x-rays as an ulcer or something—and the next minute he was talking about enlisting. He talked about "christmas trees" and going to the university health center to get them to take his speed-elevated blood pressure. They wouldn't.

"I told this jerk doctor about pounding in my head, my arm felt funny, my chest, angina; it was like he didn't know how to use the equipment."

So when he enlisted and they sent him to Pendleton and later to Vietnam, it hadn't seemed real.

Billy always the spooky one, collecting snakes, taking everything too seriously, making himself bad luck. You had to take care of him.

On a night a long time ago when Billy was eight and Alex was ten, they had been waiting for their parents, spooking each other with stories in the dark house, listening to noises from outside, ordinary noises that sounded odd when you listened for them, and Billy crept to the curtains covering the sliding glass doors, and just as he drew the curtains open to stare into the black back yard, from out of nowhere a sonic boom from a midnight jet shook the glass and rattled the whole house. When Alex caught up with Billy in the back bedroom he was shaking so bad Alex was afraid of him, didn't want to touch him, but he did, grabbed him and hit him, a dozen times. "It was an airplane," Alex said, and Billy sputtered and couldn't talk, his eyes wide and empty. "Billy, Billy, Billy," he had said, and held his brother in his arms. Alex and Billy. A. and B.

"I want to go to Monticello," Alex said in the morning, in bed. "It's around here somewhere."

"I want to go to New York," she said. "I've got to get on." She took the sheet in her teeth, chewed on it, spit it out. "I'll meet your friend, though."

"He was my brother's friend," Alex said.

"I'd like to meet him."

"He's boring. He's at work. We'll go out to Monticello." He stood up.

"Are you embarrassed? Because you're so old?" She was sitting on the middle of the bed, cross-legged, perfect. The sheet, standing up in front of her, creased, held a wet impression of her crooked teeth. "I'm sorry," she said.

"I'm thirty-seven," he said.

"You're very good in bed."

He looked at her and laughed.

"I know what I'm talking about," she said.

"No you don't."

The highways twisting down to Monticello finally offered a side road, narrow, deep in the trees so that the light seemed wet, or even old. The road was uncommonly narrow; the car felt fat, so he was glad when he could finally park it.

"Look," she said. "Louisiana." Pointing to an old station wagon's Louisiana license plate. In the gravel parking lot under the high trees there were cars from all over the country; his California plates fit right in. They walked hand in hand up the driveway to a brown wood building where other people were waiting. A bus every twenty minutes, the sign said.

"Coke?" he said.

She laughed and pressed a finger against one side of her nose.

He tried to smile, tried to remember whether he had ever thought dope jokes were funny. "Diet Coke," he said, then followed her into the garage-like building and bought drinks from a machine.

A heavy man in a checked coat pushed between them and bought a drink, then looked around, his eyes on a big woman by the open doorway into the garage.

"You want to check out the gift shop?" Alex said to the girl.

"Closed," the fat man said. "Hey, have you got change for a dollar?"

Alex found sixty-five cents. "You can owe me."

The man looked at the Coke machine, then at his wife, now joined by a fat child who was gripping her plaid skirt and imitating her foot-tapping pose. They looked like a comedy act. The man handed Alex the dollar. "You can owe me, okay?"

Alex and the girl walked back out into the wet light. "You're not so hot," he said. "In bed."

She sneered, showing the sloppy teeth, and raised her voice.

"I'm hot right now," she said. "I'm totally hot, Daddy. Can we do the funny thing again?"

The tourists looked at the gravel. Alex grabbed her arm and pressed his thumb down hard, and said, under his breath, "I'll drive you to New York."

"I want to meet your friend."

"There isn't— Yes, okay, check."

"Don't start something you can't finish."

The bus up to the house took another winding, narrow road through the trees. "Mon-ti-chello," the driver said, staring forward; "It comes from an Italian word meaning 'little mountain.' Mr. Jefferson inherited this land from his father in 1757, and eleven years later began construction of his beloved home."

The bus stopped; the house looked miniature, landscaped, austere, slightly ridiculous.

"It's so small," the girl said, on the broad brick walk.

"I think there's more of it in back," Alex said. "Let's go."

"He was a president, wasn't he?"

They took the tour; the young woman who gave the tour, prim, in a pleated skirt and crisp white blouse, referred to "Mr. Jefferson" as if he'd just stepped out for a hundred and fifty years.

"Mr. Jefferson," Alex said, as they stood on the back lawn, "will be right back."

The man in the checked coat was standing beside them, holding a nickel by the edges, between his thumb and forefinger.

"See?" the man said, holding the nickel out for Alex. "It's this side of the house."

Alex nodded. The man's fingers were so steady he could read M O N-T I C E L L O under the impression of the house on the coin.

The girl strained to look and the fat man held the nickel out to her.

"I see it."

For a second Alex was jealous.

"You keep it," the man said, giving her the nickel. "It's really your father's nickel anyway."

Alex borrowed the man's camera and the girl sat on the wide steps, in front of the white pillars and the big white door, below the dome. He walked backward across the grass with the camera, until he got the dome in the viewfinder, twisted the lens back and forth. The girl broke into pieces in the viewfinder, in the prism at the center. Alex felt the man's hand on his shoulder. He touched the shutter release.

"We've got to catch the bus," the man said. His wife and child had appeared.

Alex handed him the camera.

"I'll send you a print; have you got a card?"

Alex got out his wallet, picked a card. State Farm, Santa Cruz. They smiled at each other, and the man hurried after his family.

Alex turned to the girl, looking at her blue eyes, dull hair, freckles, bones. "Let's get out of here," he said. "We can walk."

They walked fast across the lawn, through the trees, down the hill, found the parking lot and the car.

"I don't know why you're in such a hurry," the girl said.

"Jefferson isn't coming back. I feel like torching the place," he said. "I want to get away from the feeling."

"I knew you had feelings," she said, watching him unlock the car door. She bounced in and slid across to get the lock on the driver's side.

On the way back to the motel he got in the wrong lane and ended up driving, at fifteen miles an hour, through the back streets of Charlottesville. The middle of the afternoon: no one around, laundry, bleached out on clotheslines, dead trucks in gravel driveways, bright new tricycles.

"Matinee," the girl said, back at the motel. She stripped off her clothes and left them on the carpet. His clothes were over the back of the chair. From the bed he watched her in the mirror above the counter where the two sinks were.

"I don't need this," he said. "I need a drink."

She laughed and brought the night's bottle and a plastic cup, came to the bed and made love to him and when she bit him, he hit her, slapped her hard, and rose up on his elbow and looked at her. She was surprised.

"Close your goddamn eyes," he said. "Don't bite."

"Yes, Daddy."

When he couldn't stay hard, he closed his eyes and imagined Billy, concentrated, and whispered in the girl's ear. "You little son of a bitch."

Afterward he lay back on the bed and didn't listen to her and thought about California.

When he told her, she said, "What's in California?"

"Friend of mine."

"What about—"

"There's nobody in Charlottesville," he said. "I made it up. You wanted a reason."

"Your brother?"

"He was real."

"Alex," she said. "Why California?"

"It's eight days' drive."

"That's no reason."

"Yes it is."

"You're married, aren't you?" she said, squeezing him in her small, rough hand. He watched the blue W-shaped veins below her knuckles until he almost passed out, but he didn't hit her again. She let go.

It took him a minute to recover. "No," he said. "I've got a job."

"What do you do?"

"I work," he said. "That's what we all call it. I could take care of you."

She didn't get back in the car, just took her bag and her leopard-print underwear and bounced up the highway carrying the duffel bag on one hip. When he caught up with her, she said, "I'm going to New York," and he said, "It's cold and dirty; I don't want you to go," and she said, "I wish you luck, Alex," and he said, "We'll stop in Reno and get married or something." She laughed.

So he walked back to the motel, slammed the trunk, got into the Oldsmobile and headed west, on 64. For two hours in the empty car he talked to her, told her things, like, Nobody goes to New York any more, haven't you heard? and, Quit this Daddy stuff, it gives me the creeps, and, We'll have a stupid house and a stupid garden, plant a lot of stupid flowers, you know the names of some stupid flowers?

Billy and six other guys were on some kind of patrol, they said, too late to get back so they slept in a crater surrounded by jungle, a shallow but perfect circle that still smelled of the explosive and the guy on watch fell asleep sitting up. They never woke up. At least, Alex hoped he hadn't, that his hard, perfect blue eyes never opened, but Alex didn't know whether or not you woke up when your throat was cut, just one of the things he didn't know and didn't know how to imagine, and he knew the girl didn't know, she didn't know much, even less than he did, this stupid girl whose happiness you could buy for a nickel, who was going to get hurt.

Just the other side of Roanoke, riding behind a drunk weaving in and out of lane in a little silver Japanese sedan, he saw an exit and took it, turned the big Oldsmobile around, heading back where he'd been, back through the breath-taking, innocent western Virginia countryside, thinking, You like reasons, okay, I've got some, some good ones.

Roses, he thought. Iris. Geraniums. Impatiens. Phlox. There's one called phlox.

Their House

Just like everybody else, I make mistakes, and the one I've made tonight is bowling 207, one pin better than Tom's best score in the month or so since he and Jennie and I took up bowling. We spend a lot of Sunday evenings together, usually ending up at their house. Lately we've been going bowling, because Tom used to be some kind of super bowler.

"It was the Mexican food," I say. "Feed me enough grease and I become someone else. Superman."

"Give up, Danny," Jennie says.

Earlier she looked like she wished she was somewhere else, but now Jennie's sort of draped on Tom on the couch, watching with an amused, sexy smile. Her eyes are a deep green. The smile is sexier than usual, but I attribute it to the hour and the alcohol.

Tom's just now getting over my 207, although I've already called it a "fluke" and a "miracle." Which it was—I've never broken 200 before, and rarely come close.

"You understand," Tom says. "We're going back. Tomorrow. Morning. I think they open at six-thirty."

"Tom!" Jennie says. "You're being a big—"

"I think you fooled with the computer," he says. Bowling alleys score with computer displays now, instead of pencil and paper. Tom can't get over it.

"Tom!"

"When I was a kid," he says, "my little brother—Lindsey—would beat me at everything. I never took it very well. We'd play Clue, and when he started winning, I'd accidentally kick the board over. Or Monopoly. The houses and hotels used to fall, I'm telling you." He shakes his head. "You want another beer?" he says, getting up.

"No," I say. "I've gotta go."

"Maybe I've been a little touchy," he says.

"Now, Danny, you've seen the real Tom," Jennie says. "Mister sportsmanship."

"C'mon," he says. "I was joking."

To me she says, "He was apoplectic when he saw you could top 206. He was staring so hard I thought he might knock the pins down by ESP."

"*That's* what happened," Tom says, disappearing into the kitchen. "ESP."

The living room is big, full of ordinary furniture—two white couches, end tables, a recliner, TV, and the small black garage-sale armchair Jennie calls "Danny's chair." The room is badly lit and there are slick spots in the texturing of the Sheetrock walls. I helped Tom sheetrock right after they moved in here two years ago; neither of us knew what we were doing. It's a suburban living room. Ordinary. Still, it's so comfortable I don't want to leave.

Tom comes back with a beer. "Considering that it was *my* ESP . . ." he says, and settles back on the couch under Jennie's arm.

I pick up my car keys.

"Hey, don't leave," he says.

"Got to."

"Well, okay," he says, disentangling himself from Jennie. "I'll walk out with you." She smiles at me. I say good night, and Tom and I walk out the kitchen door.

In the open garage, he has a third car, an old Triumph roadster, which hasn't run for a while. We stand beside it, looking at a clear night sky.

He's smoking. "Sorry," he says. "For acting like a teenager." He drops the cigarette on the concrete, steps on it, then groans as he picks up the butt. "I've got too much on my mind." He's stopped smiling. "I'm in trouble, Danny. I need to talk to you. I need to talk to somebody. Whenever." He flips the cigarette butt over onto the tall grass of his neighbor's lawn. "Someday," he says, "I'll learn to not pick things up. To just leave them."

I drive home thinking about Tom, and about Jennie, five years ago. Everybody makes mistakes.

A few days later when I call Tom to go bowling again, he can't. He doesn't say why.

"But I'm glad you called," he says. "I want you to do me a favor."

"Name it."

"Do you know a good bar? Rock-'n'-roll bar? Kid's bar?"

"The Solo."

"Yeah, that's the only one I know, too," he says.

"Is that the favor?"

"No," he says. "I want you to cover my 315 tomorrow. It's eight o'clock. Give them a quiz and let them go. Quiz is in my box, at the office."

"Okay." I'm in my living room, and I notice something out the sliding-glass doors. There's a neighborhood kid in my backyard with what looks like a rifle. "Eight in the morning?"

"I told you it was a favor," Tom says, and then he says goodbye and I hang up.

The kid is tramping around an elm tree next to the fence at the very back of my lot, staring up into the branches. He stops, aims the pellet gun, shoots, and a blue jay flutters down out of the tree, into the English ivy along the fence.

I never liked blue jays much, always thought of them as sort of arrogant and bitchy. Still, as I walk out and across the lawn, I'm getting madder and madder. The kid, who lives a few houses down, sees me coming and takes one step toward home, then stops because there's a hurricane fence in the way and he knows he'll never make it.

"Hey."

He doesn't move, just cocks his hip and sneers a little bit. It's seven o'clock and the light is fading.

I grab his shoulder and push him over to where the bird is lying in the ivy. The blue jay is not a blue jay. It's some kind of starling. I think, He never dreamed he would hit it. On its back, the bird ruffles some feathers at the edge of a wing. The look in its eye says it's all in.

"Kill it."

The kid is sweating and bright red. He fumbles a pellet. I take the little rifle from him, load it with a pellet he gives me and hand it back, and he shoots the starling in the head. Then I push and shove him across my yard. He throws the pellet gun over the hurricane fence and climbs after it. The gun sticks upright in my neighbor's yard. Over the fence, he grabs it and runs.

"Don't come back."

A half-hour later, I'm sitting in my living room with a beer, and the telephone rings. The kid's mother.

"My ex-husband is a lawyer," the woman says, "and he doesn't take too well to people who beat up on children. When he hears about this, you'll have cops all over you. The child's got bruises. We're going to put you where you belong, do you, do you savvy?"

"Ma'am, I'm sorry. He was— I didn't know what else to do." There is silence. I hang up, thinking, Bruises? He can't have bruises.

It's dark. I sit in my neat, empty living room and remember killing things when I was a child. I killed things with BB guns, slingshots, bows and arrows. I put things in jars and they died. I poured boiling water down holes to get things to come out. As I sit there, it seems like my whole childhood was spent killing.

It was when she said "cops" that she got to me. I try to think about something else. I can't. I think of calling Tom back and telling him the story and how he'd say "Nothing will happen" or make jokes about it. But when I call, the phone rings and rings. It doesn't make any sense. It's Thursday night. I hang up.

On Tuesday, three-thirty in the afternoon, I'm on a bench on the west plaza, watching students walk by in their running gear. I'm already through for the day. Ten feet away there's a squirrel staring at me, with his hands in his face—he's making a suggestion. So I go into Reed Hall and buy some peanuts.

When I get back and sit down, he jumps on the bench and runs up to me, stopping a careful eighteen inches away.

The squirrel eats the peanuts in thirds, watching me the whole time, cuts his distance to sixteen inches. He has a potbelly. His tail's balding. The salt will give him high blood pressure, I think, but then this squirrel's probably eaten so many peanuts he's too far gone to worry about. I eat the rest of the peanuts myself.

The squirrel runs away down the bench, across the pebble-grain concrete and up a tree, flops out of sight in the vee of a limb. Tom walks up and sits beside me on the bench. "Am I interrupting something?" he says. "Your therapy?"

"It's over. How are things?"

I tell him about the kid and the starling, and the kid's mother and her cops.

He frowns. "What did you think? They're going to send Francis of Assisi to Joliet? Terrible PR for the police department."

"It was a bad day. I'm over it now." I look up, but he's staring down at the concrete. "Tom?"

"Should've broken his neck," he mutters. He's quiet for a minute, then says, "I am good-looking. Aren't I? Danny? And honest, loyal, and kind?"

"All the above."

Someone waves to him, but Tom doesn't see, he's still looking down. When he turns toward me, his eyes look dark. "That's what I thought," he says.

"There is a problem," I say. "And it is?"

"It is tacky," he says, and laughs. I nod, and he goes on. "It's just Jennie. She's screwing somebody at work. Some political twit."

I close my eyes and try to think, shake my head.

"He's twenty-two years old. Jennie says you had him in a class once. Name's Kunkle, or Dunkle, something like that."

"I don't—"

"We have these dreary conversations. She says 'us' and I wonder which 'us' she's talking about. The best times are when I'm just tired of her. And it." He waits for me to say something, and when I don't, says, "The rest of the time I feel like somebody dropped me in the blender."

Tom is tall and blubbery, and honest, loyal, and kind. Once somebody who knew him years ago told me he was "a mean sonuvabitch."

He supposedly knocked a guy off an oil rig, out in the Gulf, and the guy drowned; that's what the story was. Somebody told me that at a party. I was drunk. It was incomprehensible. I had forgotten it.

We are sitting side by side on a bench at the edge of the concrete plaza and he's telling me about his wife's love affair. He is my friend.

"I feel like killing her," he says.

"Don't," I say, and he looks at me.

I call Jennie and make an appointment. She says, "I was going to call. I want to talk. You know what it's about."

Jennie and I met when I first came to teach here, before I knew Tom. I volunteered for the Carter campaign, mostly to get out of the house. She was running the county organization. We were in love for two weeks. Three weeks. It was a mistake.

Her office is downtown, in a storefront, the windows plastered with posters from which her boss smiles out over his Adam's apple. He looks like Ichabod Crane on amphetamines. I park and go in.

Her office is in the back, with no windows. The walls are covered with more of the posters, intermingled with newspaper clippings and bumper stickers.

Sitting behind a desk full of papers, she watches me stare at one of the posters, then says, "Yeah, not exactly Mister Charisma, is he?"

"But can he slam dunk?"

She laughs. "He's got connections you wouldn't believe. His connections are going to put Terrell in the Senate next year. I hope. I'll be glad when we lose this one and I can get out of here. It's a dungeon." Her black hair shines.

Someone knocks on the door, but when Jennie says "Come in," nothing happens.

She laughs again, a pretty laugh. "They said, 'We need him, Jennifer, we know it's a thankless job.' I said, 'Just right for a woman.' You say anything about women, liberals just fold like a tent. On the other hand, I ended up with the job."

She tells me Tom is going out with a student and acts surprised I didn't know. She doesn't know which student. "It's a rebound thing," she says. We talk about politics, how many volunteers she has. Finally she opens a drawer in the desk and takes something out, a yellow rose with a four-inch stem. She lays it on some papers. "I'm having a hard time getting to the subject."

"No comment," I say, and then I remember that this is the conversation I came for.

"You haven't been asked to comment. Yet."

"Right."

"I just sort of fell into it," she says. "And all of a sudden Tom rediscovers this passionate interest in me. It's a mess. But it happens, as you ought to know."

I slide my chair back. The floor is linoleum, scarred and dusty. "Jennie, what do you want me to say? Is this just for the record? Or do you want my opinion?"

In the dim light, she looks wonderful. The rose doesn't look good though. The yellow is gaudy, but the petals are bruised, and it looks as if it's never quite opened and isn't going to. She's staring.

"That's a sorry-looking rose."

"I don't care," she says.

A couple days later, sitting on the plaza in the sunshine, I find out which student Tom's going out with. Sarah Kenna walks up and asks, nervously, to sit down. I've never seen her nervous before.

Sarah Kenna is black and six feet tall. Although that bothers everyone else, it doesn't seem to bother her. She's happy. She sings in a rockabilly band. Every year there are one or two or three spectacular young women in the new crop of students arriving at school. Four years ago, it was Sarah. We sit in the sun. She's wearing white capri pants and glossy black spike heels.

"We're going to California," Sarah says.

"Good." I assume she means the band, the "we" that music people always talk about. I'm looking for my squirrel, but he doesn't seem to be around. It's between classes, a lot of people are on the plaza. Sarah's jittery.

She's playing her left palm with the fingers of her right hand, like a drum. "Things are starting to happen with the band. We got a new lead. Also I'm singing better. We always had the look; we just never had the sting. And I'm singing better. It's because of something Tom told me. The fat man."

She looks for a reaction when she says "Tom," her eyes narrowing in a smile. "He told me to stop being perfect and start trying to come close. Honky crap, maybe, but hey, I'm singing like, brand new."

"Tom has a touch, sometimes."

"It's a love thing," she says. "It's not just that the woman is walking on him?" She puts her hand lightly on my arm, takes it away. Right now, she looks ordinary.

"I don't know, Sarah."

She looks at me, abruptly, and says, "Hey, you don't have any old sixties stuff in a closet somewhere, do you?"

"You mean like a Fugs record?"

"Hey, clothes. Paisley ties. Motorcycle jackets. Stuff like that." She stands up, starts swaying just a little.

"Motorcycle jackets were earlier. The fifties."

"Fifties, sixties, hey," she says, does a little shimmy, and walks away, looking back over her shoulder, quickly, for effect.

Tom's not around school much for a couple weeks and I start wondering about him, until I get a telephone call one Saturday around noon.

"What're you doing?" he says.

"Nothing much. I just got up."

"Hey, good, then you'll be glad to help. I need you, boy. I'm getting the Triumph in shape. It's been in the garage eight months now, I figure it's time for some top-down motoring. I'm doing the clutch." My phone makes an odd, rapid-fire crackling noise. "Take about an hour."

"I've heard that before."

"No kidding," he says. "Would I lie? You just hold the transmission up in the air while I switch old for new. And keep me company."

When Tom says something will take an hour, it usually takes two, or more. When I get to their house, he's got the car, the old roadster, up on four jack stands, with the top down and the interior—seats, carpets, and what looks like a thousand screws—all set out neatly on the garage floor. The car looks helpless with all four wheels off the ground, like the cat going over the cliff in a Tom & Jerry cartoon. He's under it.

"Hey, don't ever go to a parts place on Saturday morning," he says, from underneath the car. "They're three deep at the counter and it's macho city. Brings out the worst in the clerks. There I was, eye to eye with a killer teenager, him asking whether I wanted the Sheffield or the Borg and Beck. Daring me to pick the wrong one." He slides out, gets a red rag out of the passenger compartment, starts wiping away grease.

"Which one did you get?"

"Sheffield," he says. "It sounded more British."

"Was it the right one? What's a Sheffield?"

He nods. "Pressure plate."

I look out from the open garage. Up and down the street people are hacking away at their lawns with mowers, electric hedge trimmers, weed eaters. Some have sprinklers out—whirling, waving, or putting out a constant fine spray. It's Saturday.

"I've been worried, Tom. I've covered for you at school as much as I can."

"Not to worry," he says. "Get yourself a beer. In the ice box. Get me one, too, would you? We're about twelve bolts from having this mother outa here."

I go in through the screen door. A couple flat, square boxes sit on his kitchen table next to a copy of the local punk-rock newspaper and a carton of cigarettes. The boxes are heavy cardboard, brown, red and black, with the printing reversed out. One says "Sheffield." Two brown grocery bags full of garbage are on the floor in a corner and something smells a little ripe. Fast-food cups everywhere. In the living room, a beer bottle looks like one I left there three weeks ago.

Looking into the living room and down the hall toward the other end of the house, I feel like a ghost, playing Monopoly, getting drunk, watching football on TV. "Jennie," I say, but I know she's not here because her car's gone.

Back in the garage, I hand Tom his beer. We look at the car. It has spiderwebs on it, around and below a headlight, behind one of the tires. He drops his cigarette and steps on it. The telephone is ringing inside and Tom looks down at his hands; the beer bottle is already filthy.

"You want me to get it?"

"Forget it," he says. "It's probably for the lady of the house. It's probably the football team." He looks at me like he doesn't know who

I am, just for a few seconds, then shrugs and goes for tools set out next to the bucket seats, behind the car. After a while, the ringing stops.

"Clutch is no big deal," Tom says. "You could do it in ten minutes if you didn't have to pull the gearbox."

While he works, he talks about open-end wrenches, which he doesn't like, and British engineering, which he does.

"British take a real casual attitude," Tom says. "If something doesn't quite fit, they just bend it. Car's got three mufflers on it because when they first imported it, it was so damn loud with this bored-out four in it, nobody could stand to drive it. You know, Throw a couple more mufflers on it, mates. The Yanks won't notice. It's Band-Aid engineering. Very funky. Goddamn," he says, as a wrench hits the concrete and clanks. "Slide me the damn ratchet, will you?" After he gets it, he says, "I'm talking too much?"

"No," I say. "I was thinking that if you don't have a person to talk to, you talk to the hardware. You know, 'Hi starter, hi washer—' "

"On Donder, on Blitzen—" Tom says.

My job is to help maneuver the transmission back and out of the car once he gets it loose, and then later, help put it back. Tom works from underneath and I stand on the bare floorboards where the seats usually go.

An hour later we have the transmission, carpets, and seats back in, and the little green car back on the concrete. Tom puts some purple stuff in the side of the transmission with a turkey baster. "Gear oil," he says. "Get in, we'll see if it worked."

When a big sedan flashes its headlights at us, Tom makes a hard left turn onto the first side street, throwing me against the door. "Radar trap," he says, tapping the corner of his windshield. "My inspection sticker's expired. License plates, too."

We stop for gas and head out on an empty highway. He hands me sunglasses, the wind gets you in the eyes. It's hilly country and there are white limestone cliffs rising up occasionally on both sides of us, where the road was cut through.

"Clutch's a little grabby," he shouts, over the pounding engine. "Should have had somebody machine the flywheel. But hey. No time." Every bump the car hits practically throws us out onto the pavement. Tom has this idiotic grin on his face.

"It's a love thing," he says. "We're going to L.A., sweet Sarah and me." The car's lurching along at seventy or eighty, I can't tell exactly which because the speedometer needle wanders.

"Does Jennie know?" I say, instantly regretting it, because he turns and stares.

"It's much too late for that," he says, glancing back at the road. "You can have her, after that teenager's through." He looks up, over the windshield, laughs. "Jennifer's done some talking. Drivel mostly, but some interesting things. Historical stuff. Guess what she told me."

He watches me until the car drifts over the divider dots between lanes. He jerks it back. I look at the dash. It's walnut. Black gauges with chrome rims: AMPS, FUEL, OIL, TEMP, MPH, RPM. Tom slows, turns the car around, and heads back toward town. For a long time he doesn't say anything, until we're back on city streets.

"Why'd you have to screw her, Danny?" He waits, downshifts, the transmission growls. "You do know how to keep a secret, I'll give you that."

"It was five years ago," I say. "It was a mistake. It was before I knew you." Suddenly, strangely, I want to have a fistfight.

"So what? You knew she had a husband." He pulls into the driveway behind Jennie's little blue station wagon.

"So what are you going to do? Kill me? You moron. You idiot."

"Passed through my mind," he says. "You know, she came home one afternoon, I could smell the kid's sweat on her. I didn't think of him. I thought of you." He shuts the engine off, looks at me, shakes his head. "You never mentioned it."

We get out on opposite sides of the car, stand looking at each other for a minute, then Tom turns and heads into his garage.

"Hey!"

He doesn't turn, just jerks the kitchen screen open and lets it slam behind him. The screen has a big long spring on it, at the bottom. It always slams.

I walk down the driveway and over to my VW parked at the curb, look back at the house. "C'mon," I say. Talking to the car.

Beach

At a Chevron station in Lafayette he had been kneeling beside one of his back tires, reaching in to pull away some of the mud and weeds that the car had picked up when they went off the road, when he heard a woman crying. He looked around and there she was, standing rigid in a delicate blue dress on the curb that ran out beside a dumpster and on to the highway service road, with her long, rough black hair, some of it held by clips, and her broad flat unlined forehead, wet expressionless eyes, one arm hanging dead by her side and the other one holding purse, scarf, and in her fingers something which every once in a while she brought to her cheeks, trying to apply makeup to repair the damage from her tears but making instead a pink mess below her eyes. She stood, and, except for the ritual dab to the face, did not move, the whole time he and Lissa were at the station, and no one else took any notice of her. Scott could not stop looking, but the woman ignored him, just as she ignored other people walking by with credit cards held out in front of them, a scruffy guy kicking a tire around to the dumpster, and a little boy who wanted a quarter for the vending machines. Driving out, watching her in his rearview mirror, he had thought he'd seen her head turn slightly after them, but by that time it had gotten so weird that she seemed as much a mirage as the glassy water on the highway before they'd hit the storm. Lissa had seen her, but had only looked at him and said, "Well . . . " and stared out the windshield.

He knew, as he sat now with his feet up on the railing, that he should not be looking out at the ocean and the dark beach before it, thinking about some gas station two hours back down the highway. He shouldn't be thinking at all; he should be looking at her legs.

"You awake?" Lissa said, and laughed. She leaned out with her hands on the railing, looking at the empty beach.

She was standing, wearing one of his shirts, and when the wind came, her nudity made him uncomfortable, although the beach was far enough away that the few swimmers and the solitary walkers with their hairy dogs at whose appearance along the shoreline he would always point and say "Look. A Kennedy," these rare intruders couldn't see the darkness between her long thin legs, they probably couldn't tell whether she was a man or a woman, they could only see lights, and people on the balcony of the ramshackle old house on stilts and envy them, imagining their luck.

"My first adultery," she said, and shook her head. "My husband doesn't care; my lover can barely stay awake. This isn't the way I'd thought of it. We are going to make love?"

He nodded. "We just arrived this afternoon, Lissa. It was a long drive. Five hours." They'd laughed about it afterward, but he'd run through his whole childhood while sitting rigid and stupid behind the wheel as the little car had spun and slid across two lanes of wet highway and parked itself backward in the mud. There was something childish about spinning, about floating backward at sixty miles an hour, wondering. "You may be used to landing on the median, but I'm not."

"Don't start out lying to me," she said. "Lie later."

He looked up.

"It's her, isn't it?" she said. "The statue? I saw it. She was beautiful. Not beautiful, but there was something—"

"She was just some woman."

"Me too."

"Maybe I should get drunk."

"Jesus, thanks a lot." She was standing on tiptoe, her long runner's legs stretched, soft hollow at the side of her hip, where the white shirt curved up. "There's no hurry. Let's think about it for another ten months." She frowned. "I'm not slinky and beautiful enough? I don't inspire you?"

"It's because you're slinky and beautiful."

"The clothes help, don't you think?"

"I said they were slinky," he said, nodding. "You could put some on."

"I thought you meant *I* was slinky," she said, and shook her head, in imitation of some perfume ad, a nice effect. Her hair was light and "done," layered a little, waved a little; the toss of the head wouldn't have worked without it. She was thin; she ran. Her eyes were clear; she'd quit smoking, didn't drink much. He tried to imagine flat-haired girls he had known, shaking their heads. Then short-haired women. Curly-haired ones. Sometimes with other women when he had imagined her, she was in expensive lingerie, steel gray, midnight blue. This last he didn't have to imagine. He had run into her at the mall one night in December and got dragged into helping her buy Tony's Christmas present, hung around in Intimate Apparel looking for a place to look while she tried the blue nightgown on, midnight blue, cut low and crazy with lace, and she came to the doorway to the dressing room, asking his opinion, standing with one arm up and one bare foot balanced on top of the other, her toes curled under. If she had blushed, he couldn't tell. He did, though. He must have been bright red.

He felt her touch his jeans, her fingers dance lightly up his thigh, lift, and touch his face. He looked over the beach out to the water, watching the white caps which seemed to disappear just when he started to admire them. I'm off again, he thought. I'm supposed to be churning with lust. Agreed to it.

"Hello?" she said.

They had been playing, when they ran into each other in the supermarket or at the mall, at work, at parties, for almost a year, looking and touching and talking. When he arrived with a date, she was jealous; when she, or she and Tony, didn't show up, he left early. "I'm sorry," he said. "I was remembering flirting with you."

"You think I was a tease?"

"Yeah. Oh yeah. The thing with the nightgown, at the mall?" He smiled. "Nearly killed me."

"Yeah," she said, "that one I've thought about . . . oh, every day. On a bad day, twice a day. Or ten times. You had that wicked smile. You just did it again. That smile drives me the slightest bit zaza." She rocked away down the wood balcony, locking her elbows and her knees so she walked like a robot. "You don't have to sleep with me," she said. "You could just—*smile*."

"I'm sorry. Something's wrong with me. Tonight."

She leaned sideways against the railing. "Technically, a tease is only a tease if she, or he, has no intentions. Lurid, base, and delightful intentions. A tease would pretend to have such intentions but she, or he, would really not have them." She turned back to the ocean. Her white shirt was pale yellow in the moonlight.

He remembered waiting for her mornings at the office, hoping she would show up in the antiquey dress, or a certain silk blouse, and how those mornings were always the mornings she wore something new.

"This is your first adultery?" he said.

She laughed. "First that counts. There was one, it was pathetic. I was pathetic. I mean it wasn't adultery, it was revenge. Tony is very busy, if you know what I mean."

"This is different?"

She looked at him. "I can feel this," she said. "I feel this, and you feel this." She turned away, toward the line of dark beach houses stretching down the shoreline. "Okay?"

"Melissa—" He looked down to the other end of the balcony, to the beach, then to her again. Her hard, muscular legs looked thin. He felt possessive, glad she was there with him, glad she was wearing his shirt, pleased with the beach and the moonlight the clouds had left behind. In the past he'd always felt possessive after, never before going to bed, and even then you never showed it, it was one of the wrong things to feel, a lot of those. You felt it the first time in bed, and before, the first time you understood what "beautiful" meant, when you were about ten, the first time you saw the statue.

"Scott? Did you hear what I said?"

"Yeah . . . You . . ."

"I said, Let's go swimming. Jesus. Where did you get this mood?"

Beach 115

He wondered when it had gotten dark. Hours ago. The breeze had turned cool and the birds had gone and the only sounds were the monotonous crush of the breakers and occasionally the oddly curved roar of a truck on the highway. A huge moon tonight. "You go," he said.

She took hold of his hair. "Oh no you don't—"

"I want a dog," he said.

"Okay—"

"I want to be a Kennedy. I want to take long lonely walks along the beach, with my pants cuffs rolled up and my hands shoved down in my pockets. And a lonely dog trotting by my side."

"There wasn't any dog."

He looked up at her.

"In the picture. The Kennedy picture? There wasn't any dog," she repeated. When she saw his face, she said, "Okay, there was a dog."

"If there wasn't a dog, there should have been one," he said. "We'll walk all the way to Florida, me and the dog."

"Okay," she said, heading for the stairway at the end of the balcony. "After our swim. C'mon."

"In Florida— In Florida, we'll kill somebody, to get our picture in the paper or something. Me and the dog."

"C'mon," she said. "Jesus."

The wind was gusting in from the Gulf across the wide, gentle beach, blowing softly in their faces. The clean moonlit sand seemed groomed, as if the kids in their stupid trucks with the huge tires, and the sunbathers, and the families with their babies, had taken the beer bottles, and pounding music, and disposable diapers, and, in an orderly sort of way, put them in the trash. Like children, he thought. Place for everything. Maybe the clean sand itself, a reproach, bringing out the best in them. The child. Mean little animals, children. Killers, really.

I'm going nuts, he thought, and he turned to watch the long-legged woman walking beside him, long tails of the shirt flapping on her muscled thighs, this woman who talked so well, beautiful to look at and to want, and he thought of something to say. "You have such confidence."

She laughed at him. "Actually I feel like a librarian or something—somebody who takes off her glasses a lot. It's not confidence. When you finally asked me down here, I couldn't believe it."

"You stand around with no pants on," he said.

"I saw it in *Vogue*."

"You do it real well," he said, looking back toward the high beach house. "It's utterly convincing. I mean, it's scary how well you do it." He looked at her in the dim moonlight. "I mean, it scares me."

"It's desperation. You're not the scared one, really." On the wet sand at the water's edge, she said, "The wind's changed, smells like shrimp," and stripped off the shirt, shutting her eyes.

He glanced quickly up and down the deserted beach, and when he saw her again it was a moment before he realized he was still shaking his head. "Goddamn it. You—"

"This is desperation, too," she said.

Her hips were too big, but her breasts were good, full and tight, machine-made, like in skin magazines. Moonlight as good as an airbrush. No, he thought. Wrong. Not right. The sand seemed full of sharp pieces of shell. She was staring.

"Me, too?" he said.

"It'll ruin my fantasy if you don't." She turned toward the surf. "What are you worried about? You look great." Trudging through the low breakers, she shouted back to him. "Quickly. Quickly."

She had disappeared into the water by the time he had undressed. The surf was cool and things, seaweed he guessed, brushed against his bare legs making him jump from side to side as he tried to shuffle his feet through the sand at the bottom. When he found her she was floating with the gentle waves forth and back, side to side. She looked better now, with her hair wet and flat on her head, her eyes big and smiling when she was in the light. She doubled up and stood, slapped the water at him awkwardly and laughed.

He wandered farther out in big slow steps, swinging sidearm for balance, thinking, Another twenty yards, another ten, and finally reached a sandbar, which made the water only come up to his chest. Something bumped against him and he jumped and made a noise. Beside him, she laughed.

It was night now and his nose and eyes were full of the sea and the moon lit the water and the water rode across her breasts like nylon, midnight blue, and he held on to that thought, until something else touched him underwater. He didn't jump.

"Lissa," he said. "I can't do it." When she didn't say anything, he said, "A fish . . . something just . . . "

"That's part of it," she said. She threw seaweed at him. "This is the goddamn *ocean*."

"No it's not."

She lifted water in her palm. "It's not?"

"No, it's not. This is movies. This is something you read in—"

Her hand caught him under the chin, clumsily. The water hit his eye full force, and for a minute he couldn't see.

She had disappeared, and he looked around, blinking. "A book," he said. He waited, but she didn't surface, or at least he didn't see her, just the water throwing him easily from side to side and up a little, then down a little, and all at once the world seemed gigantic, stars, the water, the dim lights from the highway beyond the narrow strip of beach houses, the black horizon opposite, the white moon. The rented beach house with the car underneath seemed very far away. He felt weightless and empty and began to remember things, the things he owned, a house and a car, a job and, something else . . . TV . . . books . . . clothes . . . a "wardrobe" . . . stuff in the cabinets . . . stuff in cans, with labels . . . corn, beans, French-style green beans . . . "canned goods." Canned goods. Yes. I own a lot of canned goods.

Alone, he began smiling, floating on the waves, lying back, and a new thought came. Maybe I'll drown. Sure, why not? Goddamn ocean, perfect place for it. He drew his arms through the water, and his hand caught a strand of seaweed. He shook the water off and held it up, looking at the tiny flecks of white in it. When he brought it to his face, he could smell the whole sea in it. He bit off a piece.

"What are you doing?" she said. "Scott?" Behind him.

"Eating," he said. "Here. Have some." He held the seaweed out to her. "It's awful." He could hear the eerie falsetto call of a gull, over the beach.

"You're right," she said. "This." She waved her hand over the water. "My fantasy. It's schoolgirl stuff."

"Eat."

She took the seaweed, broke off a smaller piece. "You . . . swallow it?"

He watched her breasts rise and fall with the surface of the black water, watched her gag and swallow, and felt the ocean holding him when he closed his eyes. When she kissed him, he wouldn't let go. He lifted her up with the water and she reached down with her hand and put him inside her, easily. They fell and she started coughing, and alternately pulling him under and pushing him back away from her.

"It's your fantasy," he said.

"This part takes place . . . " she said, coughing, shaking her head so the drops from her hair rained on him " . . . takes place in the shallow end of the pool. I think. Jerk." She shivered. "So I've got crummy fantasies." Her hands looked for a blouse to straighten, found none, so she straightened her breasts, rearranged her hair.

He heard the gull again, but it was not a gull, and he looked back across the waves and the low breakers toward the beach where two people were standing at the water's edge. They were waving white things above their heads and whistling, and one was shouting in falsetto, not words but sounds, which came in and out like the car radio on the highway late at night.

When he looked for her, they had each already hidden, the water over their shoulders, and their fingers touching as they steadied themselves with their arms outstretched. The water was cold.

A shout came from the beach, and something sailed high, catching the light and losing it, dropping with a quiet splash about halfway out. Then two more bottles landed, almost on top of each other, much closer, fifteen feet away at most.

"Ignore them," she said. "They'll go away." Her voice was hesitant and jerky. "Just ignore them."

He had been staring back toward the beach; it was his clothes the two men were waving over their heads. "Yeah," he said. "If they start coming out this way . . . " But then he couldn't think what came after.

"They'll go away."

"I hate this."

"You worry too much," she said, floating, only her head and flat hair showing above the slick surface of the water. She had started to sound relaxed again, she had convinced herself. From the beach there was laughter, and then more shouting.

"If they come, you disappear," he said. "Move parallel to the beach. Go . . . just keep going. When you think you've gone far enough, go on. Another half-mile or so. Lissa?"

"You've seen too many movies. They're probably just kids. I don't think we need a plan."

"Look. They don't know. They can't see. You were wearing my shirt. They think it's just me out here." But she had an odd look on her face. The voice which he had at first mistaken for a gull now seemed to be all around them.

"Scott. There's something I forgot to mention." She let out a short, weird laugh. "It's not only your shirt. It's your shirt and . . . Well, and a bra." She laughed. "I think they're burning it for me." She pointed to the beach.

There was a tiny light, a flame, which quickly grew larger. In the distance the flames jerked this way and that. The strange almost sweet voice, broken by occasional laughter, came from one of the men who still stood by the water's edge. The other guy was sitting by the fire.

"You were wearing a bra?" he said. "You were wandering around, prancing around, flashing your— And a bra? Christ. I don't believe this."

"I don't see what's so strange about it." Her voice had changed. She sounded like somebody, a schoolteacher, or the weeping woman at the gas station, the statue.

He saw another shape on the beach, running fast toward the water, but then he realized what it was. "They've got a dog," he said. "Shit. What're they doing with a dog?"

"Many murderers keep dogs," she said.

"Lissa—" The waves lifted them and set them down. His legs were tiring. Scott shut his eyes.

"Most prefer the larger breeds, but some keep—"

"Shut up," he said. "I don't think it's funny."

Cold, he thought. Tired. Three hundred miles from home with somebody else's wife at five o'clock in the morning floating around in the surf, nude, with two weirdos shouting from the beach. And impotent. Sort of impotent. Frigid, maybe. He started laughing.

"I thought you didn't think it was funny," she said.

He lifted his hand out of the water, pointed to the beach. "They don't seem to be going away," he said. "They seem to be still here."

"Yes, they seem to— Maybe it's a cookout. Roast dog. Dog au gratin. You're taking this very—"

"You want to take care of the situation, I'm open to suggestions.

I'm also cold, waterlogged, and my legs ache. But what do you suggest?" The waves seemed to come larger and faster. The tide, maybe.

"I suggest you stop whining."

He looked at her, but then he said, "Okay." He held his hands up in front of him. "Consider it done."

"I'm going in," she said. "You do what you want."

She hesitated, then started toward the fire on the beach, slapping the water with her outstretched arms. After eight or ten long steps, she doubled over and yelled. When he caught up, she was hopping on one foot in the water, and in the growing light Scott saw tears in her eyes.

"I stepped on something. A power line or something. Damn the damn . . . Damn the goddamn ocean." She shook her wet hair out of her face. "I can't even walk."

"A stingray," he said. "Here. Give me your arm."

"I can stand up. I can walk. I want to go in." Her injured foot gave her a belly and slumped shoulders, hanging breasts.

He watched the two men on the beach splitting, one guy going one way, the other and the dog going in the opposite direction. Then they stopped and waited. "It's a bad idea," he said. "It's not a good idea." He looked at her, looked toward the beach, and they started in.

"It was one of those damn purple things," she said.

"Man-of-war."

"Everything in my goddamn life is—"

"Oh, shut up," Scott said. "Just shut up, hear?"

In the shallow water now, the breakers rushing around his knees, he felt his wet balls flopping stupidly against his legs, and looked over at her, nude, and shook his head.

He heard the sweet voice call, "C'mon."

The dog was close, barking, its long fur wet at the tips, soggy, but the two guys were standing still, turning clumsily as he and the woman made their way through the surf. The sun wasn't up, but the light was, and he thought about his luck, about not even being allowed the darkness, but closed his eyes and felt the loud blood in his ears and his heart pounding instead. "Doesn't do any good," he said.

"What? What doesn't do any good?"

He shook his head. "Shut up." His mind ran through an inventory, looking, stretching back, past his job, past a night in Nuevo Laredo, walking through Boys Town, Papagayo's, at 3:00 A.M. with the two blonde college girls everyone else male and female was dark, black-haired and serious, past his wardrobe, canned goods, a story about putting a slab of limestone in a guy's mouth and kicking his head down on it to smash his teeth, past knives, falling, the guy upstairs blowing holes in books with his .357, past car wrecks and arguments in bars, to a time on some job he'd hooked a piece of rusted wire through his finger and stood stupidly looking at it and felt nothing, driving with one hand and bitching to himself about the stick shift. The emergency-room doctor had taken a syringe and stuck it all the way down to the bone, that's what it felt like. Tears had come to his eyes and he nearly blacked out. The doctor said, "This is going to smart a little."

He looked at Lissa, limping, slumped, beautiful. The guys were in the water now, a little closer, stupid-eyed puffy faces, drunk, not saying anything, but the dog was yapping and sniffing and dancing right in front of him, it was some kind of setter. He put his hand down to it.

They might be boys, kids, just like she'd said, and they were little, smaller than him, maybe just younger, but they were clean-shaven, one even had on shorts. Like dolls.

Scott closed his eyes and reached out. "First," he said and it sounded loud, how he'd wanted it, like a shout. He felt the muscles in his face tighten and rise. "First, I'll fix this fucking dog." His hand, eerily strong, rolled into the loose skin at its neck and he jerked the dog up, out of the water, its lip curled but its eye empty, threw it back under the water, squealing, and then fell on it, ignoring his nakedness, his vulnerability, hearing the falsetto cry, pushing it into the sand, one hand on its neck, until it stopped kicking and lay still. An extra few seconds and he let it float with the shallow waves, while the kids stared at him and at each other, frozen. And then they ran, kicking huge gobs of sand behind them, first one, then the other, dropping a piece of driftwood he had held, falling with a delicate splash into the shallow water, running opposite directions until he could not see them any more.

He dragged the dog in and sat cross-legged on the beach with it, pulled it, sandy, wet, and dirty, into his naked lap, squeezing it, trying to force the water out, and she knelt beside him with her leg stretched straight out, and put her hands on him. He shook her off, opened the dog's mouth and shoved his own deep in and blew air into it as hard as he could, and squeezed and pushed the dog's ribs and blew until it jumped and coughed, and he rocked it back and forth, wiped his face in its soggy fur.

He remembered chasing squirrels through the trees with a neighborhood kid, and their dogs would be barking like crazy, and he and the other kid running under the tall pines, yelling, and eventually the squirrel would miss a step. That was all it took, and the dogs would be on it almost before it hit ground, grabbed it and shook it in their mouths until the squirrel's neck cracked. It was a sort of amusement. Sometimes the dogs would let the wounded squirrel run, clumsily, angled down, and grab it again and let it go and grab it, until they got bored. And after the squirrel was dead, you didn't feel right but you didn't feel wrong, and the dogs ran away.

He sat rocking, holding the dead dog in his arms, and looked up at the woman, all wet hair and mouth and breasts and belly and legs spread wide.

"Melissa," he said. Her tears belong to her, he thought. Mine to me. When he closed his eyes, he heard the ocean rolling in and felt that light morning has that you can only sometimes feel, that soft, damp light which sometimes makes things so beautiful you can't bear to look. The wet sand felt soft, the breeze carried the sea smell, and gulls were coming back.

Zorro

It was a big, dark place with white walls and tall rattan chairs, full of lawyers, fraternity boys, people on dates, drug dealers, and some nights, when a Mexican band played, laughing, flashy Spanish types, and us, always us, there for hours at a corner table drinking and talking about nothing in the darkness, and the waitresses were these stunning women still going to college but pushing thirty, in long black nylon dresses, cut on the bias, who brought double Glenlivets and said, This was a mistake, to give us the drink free.

Now I'm standing in my mother's kitchen, thinking about Maria, wondering, Why don't we ever go there any more? In the living room Mother is shouting. When she's on the pills she is always shouting, after she washes them down with Smirnoff, Finlandia, Gilbey's. This is really not my job; I could be home in bed, watching the trees in the backyard, with Maria. It's my father's job, which he escaped by dying. But it's bitchy of me to complain about his shirking this one job.

"Bobby!" she says. "Did you forget how to find the living room or something?"

Every week my mother calls long-distance, usually drunk, manufacturing reasons I don't listen to any more, and every weekend I get in the car and drive down here. Austin to Houston on Friday. Home to Austin on Sunday. Three hours each way.

I spin the top onto the vodka, put it back into the cabinet, and take my drink in with me, sit on the low, flat lounge my father built. Near one end the red fabric has a dim, almost invisible stain which I've stared at for twenty years. It's where they put his head. Maybe it's not even there. Across the room, in front of the wall which is all windows, my mother sits in the big armchair, her blue eyes half-closed. There's no smile.

"How come *you* can drink?" she says, pointing. "How come? How come you can lecture Mommy with your left hand and slosh down vodka with your right?"

I look past her, out at the yard and a tall Lombardy poplar planted when they built the house. I used to stare at that, too, for hours, home sick from school. When I was getting better, she'd bring me steak cut up in pieces and a baked potato, the official recovery food. No one was afraid of grease around our house. Maria says, They're going to have to stick balloons in your arteries, eventually.

"Hey," my mother says. "How come?"

"Well it's because I don't do such a thorough job of it as you do, Momma. Look, I'm going home."

She sets her glass down on the table beside the big chair. "It's Saturday," she says, wet eyes. "I'll sober up. We can garden. Tomorrow. All I have to do is go to bed." She looks at me. Now she's smiling. "With plenty of money wrapped up in a five-pound note." She laughs, then stops. "Don't mess with me, kid, I was here before you were born." She takes another drink.

It's half past eight; the summer sun is just setting. The light on the back terrace is orange. When the telephone rings, we look at each other.

"Twitchy," my mother says.

I stand up, hesitate. "Hey, you get on the phone again, and I'm driving back tonight. I'm long gone."

"I love it when you're macho," she says.

"I'm serious."

"Oh, I love it when you're serious, too."

I get the phone in the back bedroom. My suitcase, on the floor, is yellow cowhide, new, from Best.

"Are you okay, Bobby?" Maria says. "It's bad this time?"

"It's okay. How're things up there?"

"Nine rings before you pick up the phone—it's bad," she says. She tells me what the cat's been doing, what was in the mail, that there's nothing on TV, her hair is wet. She was up until five last night, couldn't sleep.

"I'll call you back at eleven," I say.

"Well, I'm going dancing," she says. "With Jonathan. So I won't be here."

"Yeah, well, have a good time. Incidentally, who the hell is Jonathan?"

She laughs at me, long distance. Someone else's conversation starts leaking into ours, then fades. "Jonathan's gay," Maria says. "The new guy at the clinic. I told you about him, but as usual you weren't listening. I'll be back at two, if you want to call."

"I'll be asleep. Before you're through dancing."

"Robertito," she says. "Don't be silly." The other conversation comes back. We say goodbye, and after Maria hangs up I listen to a woman talking about someone named "Val," until the dial tone comes on. When I go back in to the living room, my mother says, "I heard it all," and then, "She's bi, isn't she?" An hour later, she's asleep.

Late, at quarter to three, I call my house in Austin and there's no answer, so I go out the sliding-glass doors and stand in the backyard with a drink. The ice cubes are loud in the darkness. Then the sirens; sirens all night now, not like when I was a kid. It's a big yard, and the trees are big. The poplar is old now, but in the dark it's not friendly; it's not even familiar.

In the bathroom before I go to bed, I make the mistake of opening the mirrored medicine cabinet and there they are, a half-dozen brown plastic bottles. They weren't here the last time. Three different doctors' names, two pharmacies, old dates.

Your reserves? I think. The other bathroom might be too far away?

The next morning I'm just getting up when she's coming home from church.

I get some eggs and bacon, sit at the table reading the Sunday *Chronicle*, switch to the *Post*, checking bank ads in the business section because the agency, in Austin, has just gotten a small bank. Stupid really, because all bank ads are the same, but it gives me the illusion of doing something. My mother looks like my mother again.

"How was Mass?"

"I'm going to join one of those copperhead religions," she says. "At least they still believe there are things which can't be explained." It's an old conversation, a favorite. "Pretty soon we'll receive Communion from an automated teller." She looks out the back windows. "Have you got time to help with the yard? I know you want to get back to Twitchy. Why don't you ever bring her with you any more?"

I look at her.

"Oh, c'mon, I was just kidding her. All I said was, 'It must be nice getting paid to yak with people.' She's too sensitive."

"As I recall you said some other things. The 'cheap spic' stuff was real winning."

"Bobby, I never said that, and you know it." She shakes her head, really hurt this time. "I don't remember ever—"

"Momma—"

She walks out of the kitchen. A few minutes later, she comes back. "Will you stay?" She's patched together a motherly demeanor with Mass and aspirin. With her hair pulled back in a blue and white bandanna, she reminds me a little of Patricia Neal. Her voice is very beautiful.

At first she doesn't want me to climb the trees at all, and then she worries about me climbing in boots, and then she doesn't like me kicking the dead limbs down instead of sawing them. When I hit a green one in the top of a tallow tree, the limb bounces and I slip. The air seems thinner up here.

"Bobby! You'll fall," she says, squinting, fifteen feet below.

"I'm not going to fall, Momma. I'm not graceful, but I can handle it. Me and this tree go way back." My father would've cut the limbs, dressed them with that black junk.

We do another tallow and an oak which leaves me with something in my eye and a hundred tiny scratches on my arms. I stand with her on the terrace, rubbing at my eye, point over toward the poplar, although it's really all trunk.

"That one?"

"Honey, it's straight up in the air," she says, wiping her forehead with the bandanna. "Let it be." She fades away, then says, "It was only seven feet when we planted it."

"Another shrine."

"What does that mean?" she says, angry.

"Nothing." She's staring, she won't let me out of it. "It's another shrine to Pop. Like the couch you've never had re-covered. Like the stain on the lounge."

I can't tell if her laughter is real or not. "Honey, that's coffee. You mean the stain on the end? It's coffee." She smiles quickly.

"Yeah, and you knew exactly which stain I was talking about."

"My Lord." She turns to go in. "It's coffee, honey."

When I leave, she's standing on the driveway. She wants me to look at her car again, it's still not right. I tell her I can't.

"You're not coming next weekend," she says. Her expression changes. She leans on the car and says, "He wasn't any damn hero, you know. Ruined my goddamn life in twenty seconds. And you— He left you, too."

"Left? Momma, he didn't leave. He killed himself." The car rocks when I turn the key and the engine fires. I look up. "It was a long time ago, Momma. You don't have to . . . "

She leans in, kisses my hair.

Out of town, I push the air conditioner to MAX, put on a Tom Petty tape and turn it up so loud my eardrums hurt. Rock and roll: curettage of the brain. After an hour or so, around Flatonia, I switch to Beethoven, some symphony I taped off the radio, a sort of mental intensive-care unit.

As the car rolls into Austin, I think of taking another route to the house, through downtown, by the bar we used to go to, but I'm tired, the traffic's bad, too much noise.

When I get to our house, there's an Alfa out front with the top down. Birds are eating berries in the tree above it, and the Alfa, which used to be solid white, now looks like a Pininfarina dalmatian.

Jonathan is a weight lifter, in a T-shirt, with curly hair. He opens the kitchen door, and our cat, Cholo, who's been trying to trip me all the way up the driveway, slips in ahead of me. Jonathan introduces himself, as he's leaving.

"He's not as gay as I thought," Maria says. "But don't worry, he slept on the couch." Her hand goes to her hair. She looks at me and shakes her head, slowly.

"Okay."

"You look terrible," she says.

"Couldn't you have flushed him before I got back?"

"It's nice to have you back." She's wearing a loose, light, faded white nylon dress with black swirls printed on it. One I've always liked.

"You look great."

"Gracias."

"But, listen, no more overnight visitors when I'm out of town. Okay? I'm old-fashioned. You said you were going dancing. Give me a break."

"I can't sleep in an empty house."

The cat bounces from floor to chair to the table top and I slam my hand down. "Cholo!" He hits the floor running, hits the wall on his way down the hallway toward the back of the house. His feet slip on the hardwood floor. I look at Maria, look down.

"He'll be okay, Bobby," she says. "He's not that fragile." She gets up and goes to the refrigerator, fills a glass with ice and Diet Coke, and hands it to me. "I'm sorry," she says.

"Me, too." I pull out the chair next to mine. "Sit over here and talk to me. I want to listen to you talk."

Later, when I wake up, nude, it's bright in the bedroom and black outside; moths are tapping the window. The clock on the bedside table says 3:00 A.M. Maria's not there. I pull on some jeans and wander in to the kitchen.

"Work tomorrow," I say, staring into the refrigerator for a beer. I sit down across from her, pull out the end chair for Cholo. A peace offering. He jumps up, yawns, sits primly looking from Maria, to me, to Maria. The crickets, outside, are loud.

"You shake now when the phone rings," Maria says, not looking up. "Your hands shake. Did you know?" She reaches for my beer; she's wearing one of my old shirts and the cuffs flop around her hands as she pours beer into her glass.

"Work tomorrow."

"You're a mess, Bobby. They're not happy with you at work, either, I bet. You've got to decide."

"What's to decide?"

"About your mother." She looks up. She can stare like no one else I've ever known. Brown eyes. She's Mexican and Irish. Her name was Mary, but she went down and changed it when she was eighteen. Her mother called her Maria.

I stand up and take her hand, lifting her away from the table.

"She needs help, Bobby. I have some names, therapists, in Houston; they're good people."

"Give me my shirt back."

There's one day of peace before my mother calls, drunk, Tuesday night. She's gotten the car fixed.

"Only they cheated me," she says. "They just smeared grease along the edges of the hood and wrote me up the prettiest invoice you'll ever see."

"Mostly they don't cheat you. They're usually just incompetent."

"Then I'm happy that they didn't touch anything, right?"

"Momma, when I was working for Lancaster this woman left us a VW, and I drove it around the block and then went into his little office and told him there was nothing wrong with it. Lancaster just looked up from the desk, and said, 'Well, then it oughta be easy to fix.' "

"It's a parable," she says. "She's me. I'm her. Right?" She laughs.

"There's nothing wrong with that car."

"I love parables," she says.

Wednesday evening at five past six, the telephone rings. Maria looks at me and says, "We could get an unlisted number." We already have an unlisted number.

"I'm sober," my mother says. "It's six o'clock. I'm bored stiff."

"Have you seen any people this week?"

"You mean the Senior Citizens' Picnic? Bingo?"

"You're laying it on a little thick, Momma. You're only fifty-two.

Find some good-looking man and take him dancing. Get down. It's what everybody else does."

"Did you change your mind about coming down this week?"

"Next weekend? Can't. Weekend after."

"How come when we get on this subject, you start talking in syllables?" I can hear the ice clink in her glass. Then there's silence. She says, "That was loud, wasn't it?"

Maria stands watching me talk on the telephone until I hang up. In jeans, she looks like candy. She walks out the kitchen door, slams it, and I hear her car door slam. I wait for the car to start. It doesn't.

Two minutes later she walks back in the door. We stand in the kitchen like Alan Ladd and Jack Palance. It's stupid.

"You think you're doing her any good?" Maria says. "You're not. You're encouraging it. If you didn't run down there every time— Who do you think you are? Zorro?" Her eyes get sort of flat, and don't blink. "She needs treatment, Bobby. You can not fix it."

"What do you suggest? Handcuffs? Anyway, I owe her."

"Bullshit. You don't owe her this. You don't sleep. You're always wired, or brooding. You shake like—"

"Hey, save it for the office. Some oedipal stuff, some R. D. Laing, and that guy in Philadelphia, what's his name? Christ, I'm getting advice from Philadelphia."

"There's no fun any more, Bobby."

"Jonathan's fun, right? You ride around in that little white car pretending you're Isadora, right? You expect fun?"

"It shouldn't be all grief."

I sit down. I think, Something's surely wrong because I've gotten myself into one of those arguments where the woman is right. This should never happen. I hold my forehead with my hand, start listening to my breathing. She's just standing there, on the high ground.

"I'm sorry," Maria says. "I feel terrible." She puts her hands on my shoulders, rubs my neck. "Could we talk about puppies or something?"

For a week nothing happens. The weekend passes. I lay out from work a couple extra days, get some sleep; we barbecue in the backyard, plan to go out Friday night. We even watch a little television.

Late Thursday night, after we've gone to bed, the telephone rings.

It's not my mother. It's a guy who says he works in the emergency room at Ben Taub, another doctor. "She's all right," he says. "My name's Matthew. I want you to talk to me when you get here. Don't ask for me. Just look. I'm taller than everyone else." They apparently picked her up downtown in a department store, passed out. He says "lacerations," "sutures," other things. I go into the bathroom and splash water on my face. No one goes to the downtown department stores any more.

Maria's sitting up in bed when I get back in the bedroom. "Is she all right?"

I nod. "She's in the hospital."

"Maybe somebody there can help her."

"I'm going down."

She looks at the clock. "Now?" She reaches over and twists the clock so I can see it. It's two o'clock. "Bobby, I don't want to argue. I can't take this any more."

Rumpled, bleary-eyed, black-haired. She is straining to wake up. I walk around the bed and kiss her forehead. "Go to sleep. I'll be back in a couple days. Hold on a couple more days."

"A couple years," she says. She's crying; I leave anyway.

The highway looks strange and clean, and except for a few semis and speeders, it's empty. One of my headlights is messed up, no low beam. I spend three hours with trucks flashing their brights in my eyes, then a half-hour getting across town.

The hospital corridors have an odd brand-new old look. A dozen people sit in the hall outside the emergency room, filling out forms. It's a slow night, Thursday. I look for Matthew.

He has a beard, not a good beard, thin, manicured, gray like rats' fur. He takes me into an empty room.

"She's fine," he says. "She's either in I.C.U. or upstairs in a room." He hands me a piece of paper from the pocket of his white jacket. "I'm not giving you this. You never even heard of me." He pauses to let some footsteps pass outside, in the hall. "Memorize them."

"I can remember." I'm sitting on a bed. He's standing. He doesn't look so tall. They must have a short crew.

"The top name is a doctor on the west side. He's a quack. He's got a drug clinic over there, biofeedback, mind control, Rolfing, vitamins they get out of skunks—sixties shit. Sex, too, probably, he's a pretty boy. Whatever. He gets results."

"What about—" I say, pointing to the other name on the paper, not wanting to say it out loud. We're playing CIA.

"She's the meanest, sleaziest malpractice lawyer in town," Matthew says. "She also gets results. Dropping her name to whoever prescribed all this junk for your mother will cut off the supply, at least for a while."

"There're three or four of them."

"So?" he says, shaking his head. "Tape the calls." He shakes his head again, and laughs, a squeaky little laugh. "I liked her. But I just spent six years in Guadalajara. Can't handle it. This is my bit; this is all I can do."

He takes the paper from me, tears a strip off the top, the "Rx," and hands the rest of it back. "Here," he says.

"Hey, how come everybody knows what to do but me?"

"You need therapy," he says, and laughs. The pale yellow door closes gently behind him.

They aren't releasing her, and I can't see her until tomorrow, so I find my car and leave. There's an Alfa in the hospital parking lot, and I notice two others on the freeway out to the house. At the exit I want, the one for my mother's house, I don't turn, I stay on the freeway and watch the big green signs sail overhead. Another ten miles and the roadsides are littered with signs for developer suburbs. Passing them in the darkness, I feel free. I'm going home.

Ten more miles and I'm staring into complete darkness; my headlights have cut out. I get the car onto the shoulder, get out, and somebody blows by me at eighty in a truck. The air is wet and cool. I check the fuse, under the dash; jerk the headlight switch in and out; pull the hood release. At the front of the car, I hit each headlight with my fist—nothing. Twist the wiring harness behind the bulbs. Look up and down the highway. Another half-hour, it'll be daylight. I can wait. I reach up for the hood and slam it. The headlights come on. I remember my father.

In the clear, dark countryside, I remember my father, the strangers standing around after they carried him in and put him on the lounge. There was an inch-high gap under the door to the bedroom where I was sequestered while they stood around, making arrangements, smoking cigarettes. The floor was white tile. I remember helping him replace some of the tile once, the way he patched together two pieces to make one with a linoleum knife and the cigarette lighter he used to carry, a big Zippo, and how the patch was perfect and how I was amazed.

For years I tried to build things the way he did, so they came out perfect, as if they had been made by machine. I couldn't. Every saw cut was crooked. Wood split. Bolts stripped. Paint ran.

Just once, I think, before you left, you could have made a mistake, could have broken something or left a sloppy edge somewhere, if only to let me know it was all right.

You poor stupid son of a bitch.

It's a divided highway. I run the car across the median strip and head back toward my mother.

After four hours' sleep, in my old bedroom, I get on the telephone, arrange for a nurse. Then I call the doctors. When they call back, I slip in the lawyer's name. They don't seem to care. One doesn't even call back. I call Austin, no answer. I try to read *House and Garden,* the *New Republic,* then settle for *Time,* watch TV, pan-fry a steak, eat alone, call again. In the afternoon I pick her up, bring her home. There's a small patch of gauze under her chin on the right side and a magnificent white bandage covering half her upper arm, right arm. She goes to sleep. The nurse arrives and smiles a lot. I call Austin all day, get no answer. I write my mother a note, throw it away.

"Look who's here," she says, sitting up in bed, when I go in to see her. I take a fifth of vodka. There's more gauze on the fingers of her right hand.

"I'm jumping ship," I say. "My suitcase's already in the car," which is a lie, actually, because I didn't bring one. If I had brought a suitcase, it would be in the car. "You learn anything, recently?"

"I'm sore," she says. "Like that?"

"No, I mean like it's not all fun."

"A speech," she says. "I love speeches." She shifts her weight, and winces.

I sit on the bed. "I always thought you killed him. You didn't. You're not even killing me, although that's what it feels like. You're killing yourself, though, just like he did." I put the vodka down on the shelf beside the bed, along with the name of Matthew's clinic, on a new piece of paper. "Try this place. Please."

"It's a grandstand play, Bobby."

"I can't fix it, Momma. Nobody ever fixes anything anyway. Nobody ever ruins anything, either. Patching, is what you do." She's looking at me; I'm wondering whether I'm lying.

"You're your father's son."

"Not yet, I'm not."

"Sure," she says. She smiles at me. "Could you bring the Collins mix?"

On the telephone again before I leave, I imagine the cat, Cholo, sitting on the corner of the bedspread, on the bed, watching it ring.

In the car, on the highway, watching the cows and fields and Stuckey's pass, I think, I can't sleep in an empty house either, and I try to bring a woman's face and the smell of her hair into my mind, but all I can do is remember that dark bar, and wonder what it was we used to talk about for hours at that corner table in those tall high-backed rattan chairs, and remember how she used to laugh. Maria.

Problematical Species

Ray is big and looks like a bobcat. His hair is short, straight, stiff, like fur, and he does that slow, sleepy blink that cats do. He is talking about my sister, Tasha. They used to be married. Now they're divorced, living together.

"She says she's too dependent." He shakes his head, slowly. "That's one of the things she says. 'You're smothering me,' she says. Will, you ever try to not smother somebody?"

We're in my living room. When the telephone beside him rings, Ray looks at me.

"Are you here?" I say.

He nods. I answer the phone and hand it to him. The conversation is short.

"She saw the car," Ray says, hanging up. He smiles. "I forgot, 'Oh, you don't care, you aren't interested in my prob-lems.' " He stands up, shrugs. "Well, it's not your problem anyway. Soon as I get this Brewster deal set, we'll play some tennis. Set that right. That fluke."

"I cheated you on the line calls."

"I know that. I did too," he says. "Still couldn't win."

Tasha, the next day, sits on my kitchen counter, dressed in slacks and a short, fluffy sweater from Hong Kong via Saks I bought for her last Christmas. She says it makes her look like Charo. It doesn't. She looks Vogueish. She's watching me wash dishes. She has my mother's dark blue eyes.

"So," she says, "hear any interesting gossip?"

"No."

"Let me put it this way—" She's rolling the cuffs on her slacks. "What did Ray say?"

"Ray?"

She gives me an extremely dirty look.

"Nothing much," I say. "There's trouble in paradise."

"Round up the usual suspects," she says. "He's just bored. I've been thinking of taking him to Big Bend. We want you to come. Camping."

"Didn't seem bored to me. Seemed like you were throwing away one of the few people who understands what you say."

"What *you* say, you mean."

"That too." I shut the water off, dry my hands.

"If you were my *little* brother, you couldn't talk to me that way." She slides her feet into the sink. "Mind if I wash?"

"Yes. Very much."

"Houston's hell on feet. No one loves a woman with ugly feet."

"Yes. Very much."

After she's through, she hops off the counter and slips into shoes. She yawns.

"Well, now that that's settled, we're all going to Big Bend," she says. "We've got a garage full of tents and junk we've never used. Those great lanterns, the green ones. You've got to come. You can play Dear Abby."

We used to fight all the time, when we were children, but since my parents died, and since she got old enough that it no longer mattered whether I was older, Tasha's become very precious to me. She understands what I say.

"Bring what's her name— Carolyn." She looks at me, looks for a reaction, gets one. "On the other hand. Maybe Carolyn, while a very nice person, and possessed of many wonderful qualities, et cetera . . . "

"Et cetera," I say.

They arrive on Saturday morning, in Ray's Oldsmobile, their third car. It's in pristine condition, a huge old blue 88 which rides like an airliner. I go to sleep and wake up outside Flatonia, on the San Antonio highway.

"Welcome back," Ray says, before my eyes are completely open. "You almost died in your sleep." Tasha's driving.

I look around, not knowing what for, some sign of catastrophe.

"The phantom ran us onto the shoulder," Ray says. "This guy in an old white Caddy was taking a nap. At seventy miles an hour." He imitates, nodding his big cat's head, jerking awake, letting his head sink again. "Gone now."

"Great," I say. "Glad I missed it. When do we eat?"

The restaurant we stop at looks like a converted barn and sells, as a sideline, artifacts like boot lighters and Texas-shaped ashtrays. We choose a miniature cattle herd in a barbed-wire fence with an empty pickup truck beside it, all glued to a green cardboard pasture.

At the table, Ray says, "I'd like to stop and see some friends in San Antonio. Unless you're desperate to get to the spiders and scorpions."

"I can wait."

"I can't," Tasha says.

"I told Dave we were coming," Ray says.

A waitress in a brown uniform arrives and takes our order. Three cheeseburgers.

"His old friend Dave," Tasha says, "is married to his old slut friend Maureen." She forces a smile. "I'd prefer the scorpions." She has already told me about this. They are quiet, looking at each other.

"Tasha," I say. "Why don't you make some trouble?"

"Take a walk," she says. It's not a joke.

"It's a nice day," I say, "I think I'll have my breakfast out on the patio if you'll just shoot her out there when she gets back." The waitress has already returned. "Okay?" I ask. She nods.

"I think I'd rather shoot her in here," Ray says, as I start toward the patio.

Twenty minutes later Ray stops beside me outside and lowers two plates to my table. "There's an extra cheeseburger," he says. Then, catching my expression, "C'mon, they can't be that bad?" He turns one of the white iron chairs backward and sits down. The Oldsmobile rounds the corner of the building and accelerates onto the highway.

"Nice day," Ray says.

"But she forgot *me*. I never touched your old—"

"Wish I hadn't," he says. "I thought I'd already paid for this one. About ten years ago." His eyes do the slow blink and take in the rest of the patio. The waitress comes out with coffee. When she's gone, Ray starts again.

"Guess we ought to say a lot of comradely stuff about women, about being irrational, some Freud stuff maybe. But I don't feel like it." He laughs. "Will, don't get me wrong. I believe it. I just don't feel like it. They wear you out with this stuff. I don't know much Freud anyway, not enough to fill a remark. How long you figure this is going to take?"

I shrug. "She has lots of feelings. Always did. Used to throw things. Break them." I smile, I can't help it.

"Another twenty minutes maximum," he says, getting up. "I'll be right back." When he returns he pushes the plates and cups aside and sets the miniature herd of cattle down in front of him, then pulls a couple of the plastic cows off. The waitress is back. Ray asks for more coffee. She gives the tiniest nod, starts away.

"Have y'all got any glue?" Ray says.

"Glue?"

"Yeah, you know, glue?"

She shakes her head and disappears through a doorway.

"Just coffee, then," Ray says.

When she brings the car back, Ray and I are standing in the restaurant parking lot; Tasha says, "Now that we have gotten our anger out, and—" she looks at me, "caused some trouble—we feel better. We also feel foolish, stupid, and like a jerk." She looks at Ray. "Will that do?"

He kisses her.

"He's embarrassed," she says. "I apologized him into embarrassment." She grins. "That makes me very happy."

We arrive in San Antonio as the daylight is fading. San Antonio is low and pretty but the suburb where the friends live might as well be in California. Their house is big, with a huge deck and pool behind it. Tasha meets Maureen with a lavish hug. Ray shakes her hand, is drawn into an embrace which ends quickly. Dave is another cheerful jock. Tasha and I take the car and head downtown; she wants to shop.

We browse along the river without buying anything. In one dark place full of curios and colorful dresses, Tasha asks an old Mexican woman for a *bolsa,* and the woman points to the sky and says, "No, senorita. At the mall." Outside, Tasha says, "She called me 'senorita'!"

"What's a *bolsa?*"

"Purse."

When I ask about her friendliness, about Maureen, she says, "You wanted claws or something? It's something women know how to do. Anyway, it's not her fault."

I nod.

"Big brother," she says. "You're taking this Dear Abby thing a shade too seriously."

"Just let y'all trash it? Like mother and dad? Okay."

"I think twenty-five years of unhappiness was probably plenty, don't you? Don't you remember?"

"I remember two good people."

"There are issues," she says.

I laugh, shake my head. Issues. The word has such power for her. "I said, 'Okay.' "

"You're sweet," she says. "For caring."

By seven we are back at Dave and Maureen's, drinking. Dave is round-faced and beefy. Maureen has a strong Texas accent. A slight scar crosses her temple and disappears into wavy blond hair. Green eyes. She's young and smiles a lot.

By nine we have all had too much to drink and she has stopped smiling. She is on the nubby white couch between Ray and me, taking a proprietary interest in my jeans, smoothing the slight nap with one hand while she talks.

Tasha and Dave are together on an identical white couch opposite us, laughing. The story he's telling is about college, a camping trip he and Ray took.

"We were coming back," he says, "and Ray had this big old diamondback in a cardboard box. The car was blowing steam, so we pulled into a gas station out there near Brady and he took the snake out of the back seat while they worked on the car. We're just sitting on the curb out front with the box open beside us and the snake's in the bottom, he's hot. He looks dead. Must have been six, seven, feet long, about yea big around . . . "

He wraps two big fingers around his monstrous forearm.

"Anyway, we're sitting there, tired, dirty, and Ray's smoking, his hair's down to here, and these two old boys walk up, kick him in the tennis shoe, ask what we think we're doing, and Ray says, 'We think we're waitin'.' One of them stares into the box, says, 'What you got here?' Ray says, 'Poodle.' And the redneck says, 'Stuffed?' "

Dave is almost giggling.

"Then he reaches down for it, and all of a sudden the snake jumps back, starts rattling like crazy." He slaps the arm of the couch. "The guy is by now practically on top of the Texaco sign and Ray looks up, smiles real big, and just says, 'Sure-nough.' "

"David always turns red when he lies," Maureen says, resting her head on my shoulder, "just like in a storybook. That's how I tell. I mean he's red to start with, but he turns sort of purple, like a popsicle."

He's staring at her. "You tell us a story, Mo. A true story, where you're the victim."

Her hair is soft, fragrant, getting to me. The scent is familiar. Shalimar, maybe. I stand up. "Is this the way out to the deck?"

Without looking at me, Dave jerks his thumb toward a doorway behind him. The doorway leads into a dining room with a big walnut table surrounded by heavy chairs. New candles in cut-glass holders, perfectly placed. A chandelier.

A door on the opposite side gives onto the deck. Ray shows up a few minutes later. We stand and look at the sky.

"Well, when are you gonna get married again?" he says, and laughs.

"Everybody argues."

"Not like that," he says.

"Whether they have something to argue about or not."

He laughs again. "Okay, big brother."

We leave at first light, with a cake. Maureen delivers it as we're re-packing the trunk. The air is wet. The cake has white icing with blueberries radiating from the center in lines of one, two, four, five, three, repeating. It looks French. "You use an abacus?" Ray says, hugging her.

Maureen smiles sleepily and says some of the blueberries are too large, in the center. "Nothing was open," she says.

West of San Antonio the country turns white, occasionally brown, unlike the rolling green fields coming in. There are hills and scrub mesquite and we start getting names out of Westerns: Hondo, Uvalde, Bandera. There are birds running beside the highway. "Killdee," Ray says.

Another half-hour and Ray pulls the car to the side of the road and asks me to drive. We switch places and I reset the seat. The big Olds weighs more than two tons, but it's a pleasure to drive, unlike my new Buick, which feels like one of those arcade games where the road is on a screen and the steering wheel's too small.

The highway's narrow, empty, and once in a while scattered with gravel. Past Uvalde there's a stretch where white bricks are lying on the shoulder every ten feet or so, so I watch for bricks in the road but there aren't any. Ray has gone to sleep. Tasha is watching him. I nod toward the back seat. "What's with him?"

"He's asleep." She faces forward again.

"I meant, Why did he go back to sleep?"

She looks back over the seat, reaching her left hand toward Ray, draws it back. "David. He likes David. Likes her, too. Dave was his best friend in school."

"I liked him. Except when I thought he was going to kill me. Would take him about a minute. Are all Ray's friends that size?"

"Yeah; but David's a teddy bear," Tasha says. She shows me a teddy bear, slumping, bear frown.

"Story true about the rattlesnake?"

She's looking out now; dramatic, towering cumulus clouds ahead of us. "The snake was probably a tad smaller than you have been led to believe." She holds her hands up, twenty inches apart. Tasha laughs, and for a second I notice again how blue her eyes are.

We stop outside Del Rio and eat at the Jayburger. It's a decrepit glass hamburger joint next to a vacant lot which stretches over to the back wall of an aging supermarket. High-school slogans are written on the wall in spray paint. "Eagles 3A State '72" and "Nuke Nederland."

We sit outside at a table on a concrete slab beside the vacant lot of stubby trees, rocks and dead grass. People park, give us a cursory glance, and go inside. Two or three couples split up, woman going inside, man bringing a dog to the vacant lot. Some locals, too, old couples mostly, who negotiate the huge, mechanized sliding glass doors slowly, with an elaborate courtliness.

"They ought to have a sign," Ray says. He jerks a finger toward the lot. "DOGS."

After we've eaten, Tasha goes back inside and returns with three paper plates. "A dime apiece," she says, grinning. "Cake." Ray starts to object but gets a quick look from her which changes his mind. I look for flaws in the blueberry arrangement, like Maureen said, but can't find any. "It's fantastic," Tasha says. It is.

As we're leaving, a brand new Porsche pulls into the parking lot. Bright red. A big kid in a cowboy hat and cowboy shirt gets out of the car, which looks like a giant red mole. The kid is handsome with wavy red hair and moustache, Zapata-style. He gets a big malamute out of the car and snaps on a leash, heads for the lot, grinning quickly at Tasha as we pass. The big wolf-dog is dancing. Ray laughs.

"Reminds me of somebody," Tasha whispers to Ray as we pull out of the parking lot. I'm back in the back seat.

For fifty or sixty miles all we see are pickup trucks and empty highway. The sun is bright. The road curves in toward the Rio Grande and at places the land around us turns lush and green. I lie down across the giant seat, my head on the armrest. Everything's padded.

"Comfy?" Tasha says.

Before I can answer, Ray says, "Look out. Here comes Sweet Country Red."

The Porsche is closing on us very fast, very quiet. By the time I can see clearly he's past us, cutting back in lane. The mole fishtails just a little, then he's gone. I remember where I've seen the color before. Childhood.

"*I* used to be stupid," Ray says, brushing his free hand over his forehead.

"And?" Tasha says.

"And what?"

"What happened?"

"Nothing happened," Ray says. "Still stupid." He looks down, at the speedometer. "Guy was doing close to a hundred and twenty. Your benefit, I'd guess. Flirting at Mach I."

Tasha settles against him and he rests an arm over her shoulders, and I settle back against the armrest, drowsy.

After a while I feel the car slow and hear a strange noise, which at first I think's coming from the engine, valves or something. It's not. There's a helicopter overhead, and two DPS cars pulled off into a ravine with their top lights flashing. The lights don't make a mark on the blazing sunlight, you can barely tell they're colored.

"Oh shit," Tasha says.

The Porsche is a mess. It's backward, facing us, crumpled into a V-shape with one front tire slightly off the ground, cut, hanging a rubber tail. It's a pile of red junk. The kid looks like he doesn't know where he is, but he's standing up, and his dog is trotting around the car, getting in the cops' way.

"Oh shit," Tasha says, and she starts crying.

A DPS man, smiling, waves us on by.

"They're all right, baby," Ray says, but this doesn't stop her crying.

We ride along, quiet, until Tasha says, "I just can't believe he didn't kill the dog."

"Seat belt," Ray says.

"I'm serious," she says and looks at me. I have no idea.

"I'm serious," Ray says. "He had the dog belted in the passenger seat. I saw it back at the hamburger place. Why do you think he took so long getting the dog out of the car?"

She looks at him, stares, trying to apply pressure.

"Seat belt," Ray says.

When we arrive, it's night. There is a Ranger Station at the entrance to the huge park, an old room in which sits a gaunt old man in a brown Western outfit with Beethoven turned up loud on a boom box. The old man ignores us. He's following the music with his head, slight sharp jerks at points of emphasis. There's radio equipment on another desk against one wall, and a photograph of somebody, looks like a politician.

Beethoven finishes up, the old man slaps the tape deck into rewind and leans back in his chair. "Ain't that purty," he says.

The old man can't hear well and isn't eager to be helpful, but it turns out that there isn't much at this station other than some rotting picnic tables and a telephone and we have to drive another thirty miles into the park.

"This is mean, cussed land here," the old man says, as we leave. "She don't forgive no city foolishness."

It is a clear night and the stars are very bright. We sleep in the car, at a place called Panther Junction. The next morning Tasha and I take a walk while Ray buys gas and groceries, calls his office in Houston. "Watch her knee," he says to me before I hurry after Tasha.

"Something wrong with your knee?" I ask, when I catch up with her.

She frowns. "Just Ray," she says. "I'm some kind of basket case. I complain about it once, and he's all over me."

We cross a long low rise but nothing ever seems to get any closer. The mountains are distant, intimidating. The scale of the place is stunning. After fifteen minutes or so, without speaking we agree on a tiny butte about three hundred yards further on, an isolated stand of rock which looks like it has made a mistake, pushing up through the hard ground. By the time we reach it, it's much bigger than it seemed. There is a trail leading up. Flat white stones all around.

"You want to go up?"

"No," she says, "I want to go home." She smiles. "We've decided to separate. Last night. For good this time."

I stare at her. "You're insane. Both of you." I pick up a rock and throw it. "You're more insane than he is." I throw another rock.

She laughs.

"I'm not kidding."

"You're acting like a child."

"Just getting in the swing of things." I start walking, turn around. "What in God's name do you expect? What does he expect? What?"

"Let's not ruin the party," she says. "Let's not get emotional. That's the worst sin of all." And we walk back.

Ray is eager to go and we look for a road he's found on the map marked "Primitive." The car takes the rough roads easily. After a while Ray asks, "What's the matter with him?" and Tasha says, "I told him," and he says, "Oh."

Around three or four we find a pair of crumbling adobe shacks, which once must have had roofs but now look like piles of crude brick. Ray parks the car beside the closer shack and takes the keys around to the trunk. Tasha and I go for what seems to have been the front door of the place. There is sand everywhere.

Tasha picks up a rusty piece of iron, an old square nail, asks what it is, and I tell her. "Spooky," she says. "The house's not spooky, but this is." She pockets it.

There is sand inside the walls as well as outside and walking through it is like walking through new snow. There's nothing inside but rusty cans and pieces of adobe.

"Will," Tasha says in a weak voice from the other side of a low wall. "I think you better come here. Right now."

When I get to her she points at her shoe. Under it, half-buried in sand, there's a snake which looks like an art deco garden hose.

"Don't move," I say, stupidly. "I'll get our snake man." I yell for Ray and he comes running, but when he sees what's going on he starts laughing. Tasha's leg is trembling.

"Not a problem," he says. He reaches down and moves her foot, grabbing the snake and lifting it out of the sand. "Jesus, you know what this is? It's *subocularis*. A Trans-Pecos. A rat snake, won't hurt you. Damn," he says, as the snake bites; he drops it, grabs it again. The snake is light with two black stripes down the length, joined by crossbars, so that it looks like a string of Hs.

"Goddamn," Ray says. "When I was a kid I used to dream about coming out here and finding one of these. It's rare. It's what they call a 'problematical species.' " Holding the snake in both hands, he looks at me earnestly, as if I will understand. There are ten or twelve tiny bubbles of blood in two lines about a half-inch apart on the heel of his hand. I do understand. He is thirteen again.

After photographing the snake, Ray lets it go. We set up the tent, build a fire, and sit in some ragged deck chairs they've brought, with the fire behind us, and stare out at the huge night. Before long my eyes adjust so the land, lit by stars and moon, looks uncommonly like day.

"I figure tomorrow," Ray says, "we'll move on over to the Chisos, and then head for the river Wednesday."

"I'd rather stay here," Tasha says. "We haven't really even looked around." She looks at me. "Ray can't miss a single tourist trap or the trip'll be a total failure."

Surprised, Ray speaks too loudly. "Margaret Trudeau here faints when she sees a little snake, then she wants to go roughing it. Tasha'll think it's a big success if we see Mick Jagger."

"I'll burn your map."

They are laughing. Ray slides his chair around to see better.

"I don't think it's fair," he says, "to call mountains and rivers 'tourist traps.' "

"There'll be some guy selling jars of water he says came from the river, and you'll buy them. You always buy them." Tasha laughs. "Real Rio Grande water. Nine ninety-five."

"Too much," Ray says. "You exaggerate. You always exaggerate. Why I divorced you."

"You divorced *me?*" she says.

Ray starts again but I stand up. "Firewood," I say, and get one of the Coleman lanterns and set off down the gentle slope toward some trees I saw in the daylight.

The trees are dead and dry and pieces of wood are scattered around everywhere. After ten or fifteen minutes I set the lantern on a small, smooth boulder and drop the twigs and branches I've collected. They don't seem right.

I choose a few, the best, and start a pile of small ones and a pile of large ones. By picking up only straight, dry pieces, and worrying about correct lengths and diameters, breaking some up, and watching for snakes and scorpions and cactus, I manage to make this exercise take close to an hour. It has clouded up, and the dead branches on the trees look eerie against the sky. I can hear myself swallow. My shoes are loud, scraping on the hard ground. Occasionally I hear what I take to be a small animal, but it might be something else, it might be nothing, and after clumsily slinging the lantern around five or six times, trying to see, it occurs to me that it might go out, so I decide to ignore the noises, which I'm not certain are there anyway. After a while, I'm so crazy I no longer care.

A native Texan, Steve Barthelme has published fiction in the *Massachusetts Review, Yale Review, North American Review,* and elsewhere. His stories have won the Transatlantic Review Award and, three times, the PEN Syndicated Fiction Project competition. He teaches writing at the University of Southern Mississippi.